THE NETHERS

FRONTIERS OF HINTERLAND

M.E. PARKER

DIVERSIONBOOKS

Also by M.E. Parker

THE HINTERLAND SERIES

Jonesbridge

Diversion Books
A Division of Diversion Publishing Corp.
443 Park Avenue South, Suite 1008
New York, New York 10016
www.DiversionBooks.com

This is a work of fiction. Names, characters, places and incidents either are the product of the author's imagination or are used fictitiously. Any resemblance to actual persons, living or dead, events or locales is entirely coincidental.

For more information, email info@diversionbooks.com

First Diversion Books edition July 2016.
Print ISBN: 978-1-68230-074-9
eBook ISBN: 978-1-68230-073-2

"In the country of the blind
the one-eyed man is king."
—Desiderius Erasmus

"In the country of the blind
the one-eyed man is king."
—Desiderius Erasmus

For Charlotte

CHAPTER ONE

The bridge was a tightrope with handrails. It spanned a muddy valley where the swollen tide had receded, and, though not as high as she'd flown in Myron's airship, it was lofty enough to make her stomach twirl when she looked down. The old woman leading the way urged Sindra across the bridge with a wave of her hand that made the loose flesh of her arm jiggle.

They arrived at a wooden building that was longer than the dwellings clustered around it. "It's late." The door creaked when the old woman pushed it open.

She yanked on a string dangling from the ceiling. A bulb cast a faint yellow haze, illuminating a row of cots and an open door at the other end of the room. Sounds of sickness echoed from a dark chamber beyond the door. The old woman pocketed the key and slammed the door closed, muffling the retching on the other side.

"Rest here." The old woman kept her distance from

Sindra and sprinkled a handful of red dust at her feet. "We'll figure out what's to be done with you at sunup."

Sindra eyed the rows of cots, ten of them, five along each side of the room, each covered by a tattered blanket. A bucket sat between the cots. Shuttered windows allowed only a sliver of lamplight from the village to penetrate the room.

Sindra searched for the blanket with the fewest stains, and as soon as she sat down, the woman hung a bag of herbs over the doorway and pulled the light cord. The bulb dimmed, glowing gray for a moment before it died. She locked the door as she left, leaving Sindra to the sounds of vomit hitting the bottom of a bucket on the other side of the wall. She hopped up and tried to turn the doorknob. "Let me out." She waited for the click of a lock, but none came.

She plopped back down on the nearest cot with worries about where she was, what would happen to the child she carried, and whether the ocean outside would swallow her in her sleep. The heaves of the ill, who sounded as though they could drop dead at any moment, kept her awake, so her thoughts found Myron, a reassuring face in her jumbled mind.

When Myron had spoken of flying, her imagination had not done justice to the real experience, the sensation of hanging in the sky in defiance of the earth, the tingle on her skin, the crisp air in her eyes, the panorama so wide it had stolen her breath. In the darkness of the infirmary, she stood on the cot and spread her arms. Eyes closed, she watched the orange mountains pass below, cliffs that looked as though an artist had painted them. Myron had given her such a gift—the joy of flight, of freedom. The thought that she might never see him again made her chest ache.

As the night dragged on, she bedded on one cot after another, finding no comfort that would let her sleep. Her arms dangled to the floor, scraping residue off the wooden planks, her eyes wide open to soak in the shapes of objects in the darkness, her imagination filling in the faces of the ill—only a wall away. Her stomach growled. She wondered if she would get rations, if these people had allegiance to Industry or Agriculture, or to someone else, how many people lived here, and whether a single wooden wall could keep the illness on the other side from finding her.

Sindra tiptoed to the door that separated her from the sick. After hearing them vomit at different intervals, and recognizing their coughs after a time, she counted three of them. She knelt and closed one eye to peer through the keyhole. Rays from the morning sun entered the room through the narrow lines where the shutters met. She caught the outline of shapes on the cots when a voice behind her startled her.

"Time to rise." The same old woman Sindra had met the night before put her hands on her hips. "Get back from that door."

Sindra stood up, her bones aching from her journey spent coiled in the small basket of Myron's airship.

"I am Pinkerton. If we are alone"—the old woman's voice softened—"you may call me Pinky. I'm guessing you don't have a name yet. What did people call you?" She paused. "Before."

Sindra yawned, now wishing she'd managed to get some sleep. "Before what?"

"Before you arrived in Orkin's Landing."

"Sindra. But on the rails they used to call me—"

"That'll do for now. Come." Pinky clapped her hands twice and turned for the door.

Sindra followed her outside and up a winding staircase to a workshop. "What are you wearing?" Pinky pushed a pair of glasses up the bridge of her nose as she examined Sindra. "Those markings on your hands?" She pointed to Sindra's Industry tattoos. "And your hair is a tangled nest. You can't traipse around the village looking like a Netheride conjuror."

"I—"

"Shush." Pinky lumbered behind a curtain and returned with a measuring string. She put it around Sindra's neck, marked the length, then extended it down Sindra's arm, first from her shoulder to her fingertip, and then from her armpit.

When Pinky lifted Sindra's smock to get a waist measurement, she stepped back, eyeing Sindra's abdomen. "What is this sorcery?" She placed her hands on Sindra's belly.

"I'm pregnant. Going on four or five months now."

"What?"

Pinky rubbed her eyes, muttering and pacing. "Wait here. I'll be back."

While alone, Sindra explored the adjacent room, filled with large skeins of yarn and a loom. Stacks of fabric leaned against the opposite wall next to a sewing machine. Pinky emerged through a door on the other side, accompanied by another woman covered in wrinkles and sags.

"Somerville is going to perform a test on you—to make sure you are still chaste."

"What do you mean? What is that?"

Pinky made a circle with her hand and inserted her other index finger into the hole, pulling it in and out. "To make sure a man has never entered your womanhood."

"Oh, I can save her some time. How do you think this happened?" Sindra rubbed her protruding abdomen. "Those sorry worms that pass for men have been forcing themselves on me since I was a kid."

Somerville's eyes widened, and her lips pursed. She pushed Pinky aside, and pulled a knife from her pocket. She grabbed Sindra's fingers and slashed the back of her hand.

"Ouch." Sindra tried to yank her hand back, but Somerville pressed her thumb in the blood and drew a red line on Sindra's forehead just above her eyebrows.

Pinky stepped between Somerville and Sindra. "You do not have the authority to mark this girl." She handed Sindra a strip of cloth to wrap her hand.

"I'm not taking any chances."

"Dromon will make a judgment on her. Until then, we may as well work on a suitable wardrobe for her."

"Don't waste cloth on this witch," Somerville said.

"I can always put them to good use—even if it turns out she can't." Pinky cut her eyes to Somerville and dug through the pile of fabric. She pulled out a piece and unfolded it, pressing it to Sindra's waist. "Here in Orkin's Landing, a woman has a set of prescribed garment patterns. I'll find you some gloves. To cover that defilement on your hands." She rubbed the backs of Sindra's hands, trying to smudge off the Industry tattoos.

"So, there're no ghosts in Orkin's Landing?"

"Ghosts?"

"Yeah, orange shirts."

"Only *one* ghost in Orkin's Landing, dear. The *Holy Ghost.* Never heard about no orange shirt, though."

Sindra straddled a stool next to the sewing machine

and watched Pinky position bobbins and thread the needle. Following a pattern laid out on a work table, Pinky constructed a pair of pants. For the rest of the day, and most of the next, Pinky helped Sindra sew her remaining prescribed articles of clothing required of all women in Orkin's Landing, and with each article Sindra had to do more of it herself, pumping the machine's foot pedal, watching the needle rise and fall as it stitched the fabric.

The hum of the machine reminded her of Jonesbridge, the turbines and the thrum of the conveyor belts. Standing back at her salvage station, in her mind, she reached for her needle-nose pliers and glanced up, as she often did, to catch Myron looking back at her, a silent conversation that made the work day more bearable.

"Sindra!"

She jumped in her seat.

"What are you doing?" Pinky pushed her aside from the sewing machine and repositioned the fabric. "Look what you've done." She worked the stitching out of the seam. "You must pay attention. Cloth is very valuable—and these articles of clothing, well, they *must* look like the patterns."

"I'm sorry. I was—thinking about something else."

"Here, come try on this hat." Pinky reached for a wide, flat disc topped with a white dome.

"I'm to wear that—on my head?"

"Yes, like this." Pinky situated the hat such that it sat at a slight angle on Sindra's head and gave the crown a thump.

Sindra eyed the garments spread out on the table. They had a peculiar look to them, not formed to address function like the clothes in Jonesbridge. The fabric, soft and pliable, soothed her skin, unlike the burlap, but the clothes didn't make sense. The blouse had six large buttons, three down each side, that performed no other function than to sit there for show. The pants hugged her waist and legs, making it hard to walk, and she wondered how anyone could traverse those rope bridges wearing them.

Before they completed the final garment, Somerville interrupted them, sliding back the curtain over the doorway. "It's time." Her somber face drew taut as she spoke.

Pinky escorted Sindra to a tightrope suspension bridge connecting the main hill to the surrounding islands of Orkin's Landing. Standing high above an ocean inlet full of Old Age debris provided her a view of the settlement. As the bridge swooned with each step, swaying from the wind, she gripped the ropes that served as handrails to keep her footing.

Orkin's Landing encompassed a large area of waterways and islands, visible from the largest hill that was topped with the white H---L-L-Y-W-O---D letters in the center. Most Orkinites dwelled on the main island in a sprawling, multilevel arrangement cobbled together from salvaged materials, mostly nonseaworthy ship carcasses, interspersed with a maze of tight courtyards and alleyways.

At the end of the bridge, Sindra entered an ornate room that overlooked the village commons through a bay of windows. The structure had once been—according to Pinky—the forecastle of a great masted vessel run aground more than four hundred years ago. A gust of wind whipped through the room when the door opened. Sindra pushed the hair from her face to see a man standing in the doorway, glaring at her. Behind him, the scent of turnip cakes baking in the market below reminded her of how far she'd come from Jonesbridge.

"This is Dromon." Pinky lowered her head at the man who followed Somerville into the room. Their shadows rose up the wall opposite the windows. "One of Orkin's presbyters."

With his index finger, Dromon summoned Pinky to join him in the corner behind a long table flanked by chairs on both sides. The two of them whispered with their backs to Sindra.

"She's a hexer. Just look at her." Somerville joined them in the corner. "Her witchery must be cleansed by the depths." She pointed through the window to the ocean.

"No." Dromon shook his head. "Our numbers have dwindled greatly from the rot. We need new initiates." He peered over Pinky's shoulder with his eye on Sindra and held out his palm in her direction. "And the Great Above has delivered us one—from the sky, no less."

"But chastity is a moral imperative before her joining." Somerville crossed her arms. "She's unclean."

"For now, no one has to know she's here." Pinky strode over to the windows and yanked the shutters closed. Her face faded to gray. She cloaked Sindra in a blanket to cover her up and escorted her out of the room.

At the center of the village, a stone tower acted as the hub for the network of swing bridges. They radiated from the tower, spanning pockets of water, low-lying areas, and the inhospitable skeletons of the Old Age city that once sprawled around them. Sindra looked down into eddies. Water splashed around boulders and withdrew, leaving a mire behind. A hillside met them on the other side of the valley, where a young woman tended a fire in the shadow of a four-story cluster of dilapidated hovels.

"This is the Outback. Plenty of privacy out here." Pinky opened the door for Sindra. "Chemist makes remedies for what ails, and useful solutions, but he's been known to set things on fire—by mishap, of course." She nodded to the other structures. "These houses have been abandoned—on account of the fires."

Dromon awaited them in the sparse room that had a cot, a wicker chair, a basin, a hole where she could relieve herself, and a window that had been boarded shut. A boy, eleven or twelve, with a poof of black hair on his head and a sash around his neck, stood beside Dromon.

"This is Nico." Dromon placed his hand on the boy's shoulder. "He'll come by with your meals and read to you from the holy books."

"Holy books?"

"That's right." Dromon nudged Nico toward Sindra. "You must learn the true path."

Nico reminded Sindra of a younger, cleaned-up version of Bug and Nap, two of the railwalkers she'd clanned up with on the rails when Old Nickel found her. This kid, Nico, wore a shirt with buttons on it and trousers that cinched up with a belt—such fineries wasted on a kid. Clothing that fragile wouldn't last an hour in Jonesbridge.

Pinky stopped in the doorway, eyeing the room, as Dromon led her and Somerville outside. She avoided eye contact with Sindra and pulled the door shut, locking it with a click.

The wicker chair creaked when Nico sat down. He

clutched a bundle of worn paper bound with twine along one edge.

"Does everyone in Orkin's Landing know how to read?"

"Certainly not." Nico shook his head. "Men"—he patted his chest—"are tasked with guardianship of the written word." He pointed to the sky. "Women are tasked with nurturing the spirit." Nico wore an empty gaze as he recited. He cleared his throat.

"What if I'd rather be a word guardian instead of a spirit nurturer? Or maybe both?"

Nico ignored Sindra's question and flipped through the pages. "There are seven downfalls. The abominations are: witchery, technology, mutation, sodomy, fornication, apathy, and narcissism." He glanced up to gauge Sindra's reaction. "You will need to memorize these, along with why they caused the Old Age society to collapse."

Sindra didn't know what any of the words meant except *technology* and *witchery*. She'd known some who practiced the arts of the earth. Old Nickel, the leader of the railwalker clan, was one of them, but she couldn't imagine what role witchery could have played in the demise of the Old Age.

"Any idea what the white letters on the hillside mean?" Sindra asked of the giant H---L-L-Y-W-O---D sign that had welcomed her when she'd climbed out of the airship.

"It says *holy word*. That's where Orkin found the texts."

Sindra sounded out the letters, noting the sound that each made, determined to learn how to read while she was cooped up in the chemist's attic for the next four months.

"What's wrong with those people?" Sindra nodded toward the edge of the village, where she'd spent her first night in Orkin's Landing.

"What people?"

"In the infirmary. Is it wet lung?" Sindra had never heard so much vomiting.

"Oh, them. They have the rot."

"What is that?"

"That's what happens to some followers that stray from the true way. It's the Great Above's way of culling the bad spots off the village bread. That's what the presbyters say."

"The rot?"

"Enough questions. I am to read to you for an hour each day." Nico held the papers up. "I'll start from the Gospel of Judas." He followed a few lines with his index finger and began, "'It is impossible to sow seed on rock and harvest its fruit. This is also the way of the defiled generation and corruptible Sophia to the hand that has created mortal people, so that their souls go up to the eternal realms above.'"

Sindra held up her hand for Nico to stop reading. "What does that mean?"

He scratched his head. "In school they told us it means that our spirits are like seeds and plants. Seeds won't grow on rocks. Our spirit won't grow in a life of depravity."

Nico spoke with a smooth tenor. Though he still had the voice of a child, he put Sindra at ease. Nico read a few more passages and vowed to return the next day at the same time, after his own schooling. Determined to do whatever she had to for a healthy baby, even stay jailed in an attic, Sindra placed her hands on her abdomen when she felt a kick.

When Nico did return the next day as promised, he brought a pork strap sandwich smeared with a bitter yellow paste called mustard. As she ate, Sindra schemed ways to learn to read.

Nico opened the book, a different text from yesterday's. Sindra ran her fingers under the first sentence. "That word. Do you even know what it means, or do you just sound it out?"

"'Course I know what it means. That word is *remarkable*. Means something better than other things." He raised his head as he spoke.

Sindra noted the shape of the *r* and committed the sound to memory. "That first letter, how do you know to say it like that?"

"Ahr—'cause that's how you pronounce it." Nico snatched the pages back from Sindra and began reading. "This holy book is called *Vogue*, March, 1967. *What Women are Wearing*." He flipped to the middle. "These are the prescribed articles of clothing that women must wear."

She recognized the hat in the picture right away, like the one Pinky had put on her head. She leaned over his lap as he read. She watched his mouth, the way he formed the letters, observed his lips and the spittle from his pronunciation of p's and b's, making mental notes about the subtle differences between *blouse* and *plows*, unable to tell the difference, except for the *s*.

Every day, when he finished his reading, Nico placed the book he'd read from in a nook by the window. As soon as Sindra heard the dreadful sound of the lock click shut, she reached for the book and practiced rereading what Nico had read, applying anything new she'd learned that day.

In the months that followed, in addition to reading, she passed the time learning to sew with Pinky and memorizing the canons of Orkin's Landing. Her confinement wore her down. Minutes, seconds, days—they dragged on as if one were no different than the other. Nico's voice, once soothing, began to grate on her nerves, and his face annoyed her as he read with a little twitch in the corner of his mouth.

"What does that mean? What does that say? What's that letter? Your questions never stop. Women should not ask so many questions." Nico dropped the book on the ground. "I told you already. *A* can be 'ah' or 'a' or even 'uh.'"

"I know. That's not what I'm asking."

"What are you asking?" Nico rubbed his eyes.

"I'm asking about that word, *awl*." She pointed to a passage in the book. "You say it just like *a-l-l*."

"Sometimes the other letters in the word change how it's pronounced. *A-l-l*, 'ahl,' would be a long *a* if you put an *e* at the end instead of an *l*. Making it *ale*."

Sindra scratched her head, trying to understand. "Okay, well what about *holy*? You say 'ho-lee,' and on the sign with the big white letters there are two l's and you still say 'ho-lee.' The double l's should change the way it's pronounced, right?" Sindra thought about that sign often, so prominent on the hillside. "And how do you know the missing letters are *o* and *r*? H---L-L-Y-W-O---D could be anything, right? Like HALLYWOLD or HULLYWORD or HOLLYWOLD or HOLLYWOOD or—"

"But none of those words make sense, do they? Orkin figured that the Old Age people that built the letters misspelled the words, but their mistake didn't change its meaning."

Sindra watched Nico leave, heard the lock click, and leaned back in her chair with a sigh. Sitting so much these past few months had made her legs weak and her back ache, so she began to stand by the shuttered window, peering through a slit for a glimpse at life in Orkin's Landing, and in her many hours of solitude, Sindra spoke with the child she carried, hoping to impart some of what she'd learned in her seventeen years of life.

"If you're a boy," she rubbed her belly, "figure out who you can trust." She hoped for a boy so that he could avoid all the pain she'd endured at the hands of men. "If you're a girl—sharpen your claws and get used to the taste of your own blood. The world was not made for you. Either way," she thought of Myron and his dreams of finding a better place in his airship, "never stop searching."

That night, she fell asleep with visions of Myron, the two of them raising her baby together in Bora Bora without all of the hardships and holy books and nonsense about things people can't do. She questioned her decision not to leave this place and try it alone somewhere else. But the hope of seeing her baby's face, hearing the cry, feeling skin to skin on her breast, was the reason she'd lived in confinement for four months. Out in the Nethers alone, her baby wouldn't stand a chance. Living here, resting, with food in her belly, gave her baby the best shot at life.

Myron once told her that his grandfather's name was Samuel. Samuel taught him how to build an airship. She liked the name, respected the man behind Myron's stories, so if her baby came out a boy, she would name him Samuel; otherwise, she'd go with Sam, the perfect name for a strong, intelligent girl.

When the day finally came for her water to break, Sindra labored for hours with Somerville and Pinky at her side and a gallery of Orkin's Landing presbyters who insisted on cramming into the tiny room for the show. Dromon paced and the chemist made faces.

"Get out of here." Sindra tried to wave off the crowd, which made her uneasy. "It hurts."

"I know it hurts, but you gotta push." The top of Pinky's head rose between Sindra's legs.

Sindra screamed as a bolt of pain shot down her back. Every time her abdomen contracted it felt like an excruciating stint in the stretcher block.

Since the seed of Sindra's baby certainly came from a ghost and not a slog, Lalana, the animal doctor in Jonesbridge, had given the baby a fifty-fifty chance of surviving birth. After the trials of escaping Jonesbridge and the agony of labor, the question that had plagued Sindra for months would finally be answered—if her baby took a breath outside the womb, would he or she have both arms? Both legs? Hearing and sight? Or would her baby suffer the fate of a slog birth, deformed and destined for the dead yard within the first few days?

Sindra watched the faces of the crowd in the room for signs that might hint at her baby's health. Dromon and Somerville stood behind Pinky as she cupped the baby's head. The chemist, two other women, and an old man in a robe all looked on, holding their breath until the baby slid into Pinky's arms.

The robed man stepped forward, his eyes concealed by the shadows of his hood. He cut the umbilical cord, wrapped the baby in a blanket, and stepped outside, slamming the door behind him.

"Where are you taking him? Is it a him?" Sindra tried to

sit up. "What's wrong?" She heard a faint cry from outside. "Bring me my baby!"

"There, there, dear." Pinky wiped Sindra's forehead with a towel.

"Where's he taking my baby?" She yelled again, "I want my baby!"

The crowd in the room departed, leaving only Sindra. "Where's my baby?" she screamed again when the door locked.

CHAPTER TWO

Jonesbridge had buzzed with activity since the defeat of the E'sters. Slogs worked extra shifts. The administrators diverted attention from munitions to secretive projects in the machine shop and salvage. Defense troops deployed elsewhere, leaving Jonesbridge virtually undefended from outside attack.

Myron's promotion proved to be a worse fate than the drudgery of labor. The tedium of keeping a sharp eye on the workers in his charge left his mind free to roam in his dreams like never before. After only four months in charge of the salvage factory, Myron found himself demoted back to a slog on the line, working *for* Saul, instead of *over* him.

From his first day in the admin overlook, he'd kept his eyes peeled for anything he could use to build a new airship, so he could take the same course Sindra had taken, holding out hope that they could still journey to Bora Bora together. That was the dream that drove him to take another breath, but he had other dreams, aspirations that his grandfather had once told him have to stand in place of those dreams that lie beyond reach.

With his knack for salvage and his aptitude for gears and metal, and with his strength and endurance that exceeded anyone else's at Jonesbridge, he'd always hoped the Superintendent would someday put him on a mobile salvage squad beyond the gorge, scouring the burnt earth. As the ghost captain spoke, Myron anticipated the words as if he'd formulated them himself.

"Them E'sters left enough scrap in their ruins to supply our factories for a good while. Only problem is it lies outside the gorge. Much of it in the gorge."

Another ghost stepped forward. "Our trustworthy defense teams have been deployed on another important mission. The mobile squad will come from the slog ranks. But—Civil Guards are authorized to shoot on sight for any infraction you commit out there."

Two ghosts escorted Myron to procure his ration before they led him to the supply train depot. Fifteen slogs shackled one in front of the other waited by an open train car. On Myron's ankles, the ghosts fastened iron cuffs with a slack chain between his feet. On his left foot, a chain connected him to the left foot of the slog in front of him. They chained his right foot to the right foot of the one behind him.

Myron could smell the breath of the man at his back as he drew close, and it turned his stomach.

"Watch your back, Myron," Saul whispered. He nudged Myron between the shoulder blades.

The jingle of chains grew quiet when a ghost stood on a crate to address the slog line. "I don't expect to see any shittery on the way to the rim. Keep them chains straight. March with the cadence. Stay in step."

Another ghost yelled, "If you're too stupid to know your left from right, this here is left." He turned his back to the line, raising his left arm. "And this here is right." He raised his right arm. With a deep breath, he barked the cadence. "Left. Right..."

Chains rattled as the group marched toward the train, tripping and stumbling as at least a quarter of them marched opposite the correct foot, including Saul, whose mistake sent Myron stumbling into the man in front of him.

"Wrong foot, fool." Saul slapped Myron in the back of his head.

Myron swung his arm, elbow first, trying to make contact with Saul. "*You* got it wrong."

Saul lowered his voice as a ghost ambled by them. "I see why your girl ran off without you now."

"Quiet back here."

Myron braced for a swat from a discipline rod that came moments after the ghost spoke, striking his lower back.

The procession marched up a ramp into the windowless train car. They sat in a line that ran around the interior perimeter of the car. Darkness fell over the sixteen faces that all bore nervous excitement as the last puff of outside air rushed in through the closing doors.

Myron's eyes had adjusted enough to the darkness to decipher the outline of Saul's head. He eyed Saul's profile, the narrow chin and overbite, a face he associated with betrayal, but the clack of the train on its tracks lulled him into a trance.

Four months had passed since Myron sat in the creek

bed, blood oozing from his leg, watching Sindra twist on a rope beneath the airship he'd built, Coyote Man safely in the basket, lifting into the smoke. He'd constructed numerous outcomes to fill the void of not knowing whether Sindra, or the entire contraption, had plummeted onto the sharp rocks at the base of Iron's Knob, or into the gorge, or smack into the E'ster encampment, but whenever he envisioned a safe landing, it was always on a barren mesa in the middle of the Nethers. No water. No food. No protection from the wind that legend claimed blew bullets of sand and stone. As they traversed the bridge, the sounds on the track and the speed of the train changed, punctuating the depth of the void beneath them. After all his attempts to construct an airship and all the time he spent planning, he would finally get to leave Jonesbridge, if only for the day.

When the train stopped, the mules unloaded first, braying as they plodded down the ramps of the adjacent cars. A lock clanked open, and the door to the slog car slid aside. His fellow slogs squinted, holding up their hands to shield their eyes from the sudden light. Saul glared at Myron.

"Up, up," the ghost shouted.

The line disembarked in opposite order of how they'd boarded. Each received waterskins to sling around their necks, and a set of field tools: pliers, pluckers, sandyrods, and hammer. In a panic, Saul lifted his waterskin to his mouth and gave it a squeeze.

Myron patted his own waterskin, curious as to why he wasn't thirsty like everyone else. He had thought a lot about his discovery of S.L.O.G.'s in the belly of the Stony Mountain facility and what it meant. He wondered how many of those that were called slogs actually were slogs, and how many (most, he presumed) wore the name as nothing more than a slur. Growing up in isolation, Myron never realized how much stronger he was than other people, how much faster. Not only could he outlast Saul's thirst, Myron was sure he had three times Saul's strength, as well.

Two ghosts approached the group. "There's a whoresworth of E'ster trap out here, yet. Still rotting and stinking up the place."

One of the ghosts pulled a wheelbarrow full of lime bags up to the line. "Splitting off in pairs. First thing is pulling out what's left of the corpses from the armor and giving 'em a dust." The ghost traveled the line handing each slog a bag of lime. He pulled out an iron ring full of keys and unlocked every other shackle, making eight sets of two slogs, with Myron and Saul, as the last two in line, still shackled together.

"Oughta be dusting you with lime," Saul said under his breath.

Myron jerked his leg to walk, pulling the chain that connected them, forcing Saul to follow as they headed toward what had been the E'ster encampment, now filled with the burnt skeletons of artillery and catapults. By the train, still outfitting the mules, Myron spotted Lalana and Errol and fought pangs of nostalgia for the brief time they were all going to fly away together.

"Start over there," a ghost yelled to Myron. He pointed toward a mangled troop transporter. It was constructed of solid metal with holes blasted in the side and the roof crunched.

Myron stuck his head into the half-open door of the transport. His nose burned. Inside, he counted ten E'sters, torn apart and mixed with debris, pieces of bodies in the state of decomposition where their faces had caved and their skin had turned gray.

Myron worked to remove the door of the damaged transport on the left side and Saul tinkered with the one on the right. Myron broke down the door with a cold chisel and heavy hammer. He began separating body parts from rubble and pulling the human remains into a pile outside of the transport. He did his best to keep his eyes up, not glancing down to the dismembered arms and legs, the broken faces of the E'sters, but had to look at them when he dusted the pile.

He rubbed his neck and gazed into the horizon. The smoke on this side of the gorge thinned, leaving more sunlight to bathe the parched earth in yellow. Silhouettes of barren peaks created a gray wall against the western horizon, where civilization ended and the Nethers began.

They worked, Myron and Saul, as far from one another as the chain would allow while they were dismantling the transport, but the removal of the side panel required them to work as a team.

Lalana led a mule and cart to the transport for them to load the heavy doors and other large metal scraps to take back to the train.

She stared Saul down and eased up beside the cart, pretending to work on the mule's harness, whispering to Myron. "This is Chimney." The mule's ears twitched when he heard his name. He brayed and yanked his head toward Lalana. "Youngest, fastest mule in the stable." Myron strained to hear her voice.

Saul stopped work, cocking his ear toward Lalana.

"You take Chimney." She nodded toward the horizon,

her voice so soft Myron could hardly make out her words. "Go. Find that girl." She waited for Saul to look away before loosening the buckles on Chimney's harness. "Give him a good kick." She pointed to the best spot to nudge the mule, on the side of the belly. "Then yell his name a few times. He'll bolt out of here like his mane's on fire."

Myron nodded to the shackles between him and Saul. Lalana cut her eyes to his hammer and chisel.

"Mule's ready to go. Best load all this metal up now," she said, no longer whispering.

The ghosts patrolled the work area, as expected, in teams of two, one team within earshot of the zoned work area. To the south, two slogs dismantled the E'ster command post. Near the gorge rim, another two slogs took apart a fused cannon turret.

Chimney had already begun separating from the cart, gnawing on a bramble a few steps away. Myron had to time his escape with precision. Every tick counted. He and Saul bent down in unison, each with a pair of hands on the door to hoist it into the cart. Myron eyed the shackle for a weak link, spotting the perfect place to strike.

With the first metal door seated in the cart bed, they bent for the next one. Once Saul lifted his half, Myron dropped his side and reached for his tools. The hammer struck the chisel on the chain link. The link pressed into the dirt beneath.

"What are you doing?" Saul struggled to see over the edge of the heavy door. "Guards!" he yelled. He dropped the load and stood straight, pointing at Myron, the same way he'd betrayed him before.

Myron grabbed the chain connecting his leg to Saul's

and yanked Saul's legs out from under him. He positioned the link on the metal corner of the salvaged transport door to give support underneath, so he could sever the chain. With the chisel in position on the link, Myron raised the hammer. Saul punched him the face. Myron fell back, and the hammer clanked off the edge of the cart. Saul lifted the hammer over Myron's head to strike. Myron dodged the blow by rolling to his left. Saul moved in, wrapping the slack of the chain around Myron's neck. The two nearest ghosts ran for the scuffle, but climbing over debris slowed their progress.

Myron elbowed Saul in the stomach and wedged his fingers between the chain and his throat to open his airway. Myron twisted around, winding up chest to chest with Saul, both tangled in the tether chain.

His last chance. This was it. No more shirker coop or stretcher or ceremonious execution. This time, they'd put a bullet through his head and dust him like the hundreds of E'sters littering the ground. The ghosts, getting closer, took aim at Myron. He pummeled Saul in the face, who fell limp to the ground. Reaching for his hammer on the other side of the cart, Myron tugged the chain, pulling Saul with him, but his chisel had rolled under a hunk of E'ster battleworks.

"Git, Myron," Lalana yelled.

Behind him, Lalana moved in front of the head ghost as he pulled the trigger. Lalana took the ghost's bullet and collapsed on the ground. "Lalana!" Myron ran for Chimney, both hands tugging Saul behind him.

He climbed on the mule. Saul's weight tugged at his foot. When Saul tried to pull him down with the chain, Myron kicked him in the head and then dug his heels into the mule. "Go, Chimney!" he yelled. "Go, Chimney!"

The mule brayed with a kick and loped toward the western horizon, dragging Saul with them followed by a cloud of dust.

Chimney loped through a draw and dashed over a hill as though a specter were nipping at his heels. Myron struggled to keep Saul's weight from pulling them both to the ground. The dust cloud that dragging Saul left gave the pursuing ghosts an easy way to track them.

Myron wrapped one arm around Chimney's neck and with the other he hauled Saul onto the mule's haunches. Saul's head draped over one side, his mouth gaping open. His feet dangled over the other side. Myron couldn't tell if the blows from the rocks the Chimney had dragged him across had killed Saul or just left him addled in mind darkness.

Chimney reared at the sight of a ravine, dodging an outcropping and flying down the steep slope, unable to keep his footing. The mule stumbled and brayed, moaning more in agony than in reaction to Myron's kick. Myron and Saul rolled off the mule as the jagged hills rose to meet them in the settling dust.

Chimney brayed again. Myron spotted the mule's hoof wedged in a crevice, the bone in the hock broken.

"Shhhh," Myron whispered, stroking the mule's nose, scratching behind his ears. "Please. Shhhh." He knelt beside Chimney and worked the hoof free. The mule limped forward and collapsed.

A steam truck engine groaned from the other side of the hill, followed by a hiss of steam as it came to a stop. Then the only sound was a gust of wind whipping through the ravine. Myron watched Chimney's flanks rise and fall with shallow breaths, praying he wouldn't bray. Saul's chest also showed signs of breath.

Myron heard footsteps on the ridge above him. He tugged Saul under the cover of an overhanging rock formation, but he could do nothing about Chimney, sprawled out at the bottom of the ravine. Myron rolled Saul out of the way, their tethered legs separating them by no more than three feet. Voices muted by wind chattered atop the ridge. Saul stirred, letting out a faint moan. Myron held his breath.

"Wha—" Saul muttered before Myron slapped his hand over his mouth.

Chimney rolled, trying to stand, and brayed.

"There's the mule," a ghost said. "Must be around here somewhere."

Myron hoisted Saul over his shoulder and stumbled in the shadow of the ridge in the opposite direction of the ghosts' voices, toward the Nethers, where the ghosts wouldn't go. Myron's feet landed on stones and twigs. Drops of blood dripped from Saul's head with each step, leaving a trail of blood into the Nethers.

CHAPTER THREE

At the intersection of every bridge, in the stalls of the market, carried by the breeze, and with each groaning turn of the windmill, Sindra heard her baby's cry, a delicate caw, leaving so many more questions than answers.

Pinky had told her the baby didn't make it. According to Somerville, her baby needed medical attention. Dromon said that the Great Above had taken her baby home.

Sindra had heard the cry. She'd seen the faces in the room, no shock or concern, all looking at a healthy baby. Her longing to hold her child made her chest ache.

Nico entered the room with a bowl of stew and fresh water. He sat down beside Sindra's bed and wiped her tears with a rag. "I'm sorry, Sindra."

"Not hungry." She pushed the bowl away.

"I…" Nico placed the bowl on the floor. "I…think it's wrong."

"What?"

"That the presbyters didn't let you see your baby."

"Fifty-fifty. I knew there was a risk my baby wouldn't survive." Sindra sat up in bed. "I thought I'd have a better chance here than out there somewhere." She nodded in the direction of the Nethers. "Got no reason to stay now. Unlock the door."

"It only unlocks from the outside." Nico rattled the door handle. "Dromon will open it soon."

"The minute that door opens, I'm gone."

"You can't leave."

"What do you mean?"

"They won't allow it."

"I don't care what they allow." Sindra charged at the door. She shook the handle, banged the door, punched and pushed. The heavy timber of the doorframe absorbed her blows. "Let me out of here!"

Nico grabbed her shoulders from behind. Sindra swung, missing his head. She reached for the bowl of stew and hurled it at him. He dodged the blow from the bowl, but chunks of sinew and wild onion dripped from his face. "You're just like them. I only stayed shut up in this dungeon 'cause of my baby's health." She groped for the bowl, picked it up again, and this time connected with Nico's head.

"I know you're angry—"

"Angry?" Sindra wrapped her hands around his throat. "If you see me *angry*, it will be the last thing you see."

Nico swatted her hands away and backed up against the wall. "I—well, I know where they took her."

"*Her?* My baby? She was a her?" Sindra imagined the face that would produce such a fragile cry. "Sam," she whispered.

"That's right." Nico pressed into the corner as Sindra edged closer, her hands on his chest.

"Where is she? I have to see her." Sindra had heard legends that coastal villages buried their dead by putting them in boats that leaked and setting them out to sea. "What sort of burial do you folks do around here?"

Nico lowered his eyes. "I shouldn't tell you this. They told you she died but sh—"

"She's not dead, is she?" Sindra ran at the door again, charging with her shoulder. She backed up and rammed it again, and a third time, screaming, "Where's my baby?" She slid down to the floor, sobbing. "Where is she?"

"She's all right. She's healthy."

"When will they let me see her?"

"I don't know. She's with Orkin now."

"Where is Orkin?"

Nico helped Sindra to her feet. "I don't know where Orkin lives. On an island, I think. That way." He pointed to the southwest. "He only shows up for festivals and rituals and such."

The lock clicked. Sindra wedged into the opening as the door creaked open.

"What's going on in here?" Dromon blocked Sindra's path.

"You stole my baby." Sindra pounded Dromon in the chest as he wrapped her in his arms. She kicked at his bull eggs, landing instead on his shins. Coming up from behind him, two men pushed her to the ground on her stomach, one of the men resting his knee in the middle of her back. Sindra tried to wiggle free, but the other man's hands were as strong as a vise.

Dromon nodded toward a woman who kneeled beside

Sindra. Another man clutched Sindra's bicep, choking off the blood to her forearm. The woman stuck a needle into Sindra's arm, plunging a murky liquid into her body. Within seconds, the medicine snuffed the sounds of the ocean and pulled a velvet curtain between Sindra and her world. Her arms, so heavy she couldn't budge them, tingled until she could no longer feel them. Dromon spoke to her, but she could only smell his words, not hear them. For minutes or hours or seconds, a numb weight sat on her chest, her breath so slight that it conjured images of snowflakes drifting against a pale sky.

Her legs would not move, so they carried her on a stretcher. The sky moved above her. Bursts of blackness shrouded her vision. Her heart thumped. She floated, as though death had claimed her, but instead of leading her on a pleasant journey to the Great Above, her custodian spirit was escorting her straight to the fires of the Chasm. When she stopped, a speaking man loomed over her. His voice flamed from his mouth.

"I am Orkin."

Dromon lifted Sindra's face to look at Orkin.

"The choice is yours. Absolve your unclean spirit in death," Orkin raised the palms of his hands skyward, "as an offering to the Great Above—or undergo the purity ritual and join with Nico.

"What will it be?" Orkin placed his hand on Sindra's head. "Live in the word, or die?"

Sindra shook her head, trying to focus, her vision blurry as the faces in the room spun into a fuzzy collage of flesh and scowls. She opened her mouth to speak. No words came out, only a string of drool. Her double vision produced an extra Nico, kneeling beside her with his head bowed.

"Lif." Her tongue, as though it were three times too big for her mouth, pushed the word out ahead of a mist of spit. "Live." Sindra lowered her head and closed her eyes.

Orkin raised both arms.

"Ba—ba—baby?" Sindra coughed. "Where?"

"Nico is the only man of joining age."

"He—he's a kid," Sindra whispered.

"I'm twelve."

"Enough." Orkin gestured for his presbyters to bring Sindra and Nico to the altar. "You will join with Nico, whose complete name is Nico Somerville. You will be known from this point forward as Somerville."

Sindra's head rolled toward her shoulder as she protested. "Already," she said between breaths, "a Somerville in village."

"There are four, to be exact. You will be the fifth." Orkin received a torch from a hooded presbyter.

"I can't join with her. She'll kill me." Nico walked on his knees toward Orkin. "Please. Somebody else."

"You are the only unattached male old enough to consummate a proper joining."

Though Sindra did not know the meaning of the word *consummate* for sure, she had a good idea what it meant. Ghosts, admins, E'sters, Orkinites—all had it in their heads to ravage her like a carpie. One way or the other, wrapped in dressing or said outright, consummate would mean the same thing as what the ghosts had done to her.

Regaining her lucidity in brief chunks, Sindra stood up and fell back to her knees. She pushed the matted hair from her eyes, so that Orkin could see the resolve in them. "He's right. I will kill him."

The rest of the ceremony occurred with her still in a mental haze as thick as the smoke over Jonesbridge. On the hillside across the water, a long procession of chanting Orkinites carried torches that snaked in a line. Men in black robes hummed while women in blue sang an eerie tune as they strode in a circle around Sindra and Nico. Their voices resembled the sound wind makes when it howls against a pane of glass, and their figures cast long shadows that waved as the flames of the torches danced.

Sindra had dreamed of joining with Myron someday. He'd promised to help her raise her baby. She'd risked everything, lost Myron and her baby, trading one prison for another. In Jonesbridge she'd had the satisfaction of her work, salvaging and repurposing, glimpsing bits of the past. When she lay on her cot at the end of the day, her fatigue had plummeted her into sleep. Here, she held no worth as a productive worker. She only sat and waited, so much so that she'd grown afraid her muscles would turn to jelly. Now, according to Orkin's pronouncement, she and Nico were married.

After the ceremony, the Orkin's Landing village council assigned to Sindra and Nico, as their first dwelling, a wedding hut on the outskirts of town, a one-room hovel with one cot, one basin, a stove, and a rack of wooden plates and cups. Sindra and Nico stood opposite each other, Nico's eyes on the floor, Sindra staring out the window, studying the bridges for the quickest way out of Orkin's Landing.

"What do we do now?" Nico sat on the cot and looked up at Sindra.

"I don't really care what *you* do. I'm going to find my baby." Sindra pushed on the door.

"No, you aren't." Four presbyters entered the tiny wedding shanty with a pack of chains, straps, and heavy fabric.

"You, Somerville, are Nico's wife." One of the presbyters uncoiled a leather strap that resembled a harness.

"My name is not Somerville!"

The hooded figure who had taken Sindra's baby followed the presbyters into the room.

"You!" Sindra leaped toward the man and yanked down his hood. She groped in her pocket for the star Myron had made for her in Jonesbridge as a token of his affection, something that had gotten her out of more than one jam. She held the jagged point of Sindra's star to his throat. "I want my bab—" Pain shot from the top of her head to her teeth. She bit her tongue and collapsed in darkness.

When the faces came into focus above her, Sindra tried to rub her head, but, as she moved her arm, Nico's arm moved with it, draped in fabric. She lifted both of her arms over her head, pulling both of Nico's arms along for the ride. She yanked her foot back, and Nico's came with it.

"What is this?" She stood up, her limbs flailing in all directions but hampered by the pull of Nico's limbs in the opposite direction. Her upper arm was chained to Nico's upper arm, forearm to forearm, wrist to wrist, waist, legs, ankles, and neck tethered together with Nico's.

"That is a unity binding." Dromon tapped the locking mechanism around Sindra's wrist, one of fourteen different locks. "Only used in extreme cases. But once you have sanctified your marriage, we will undo the binding."

"If this kid lays a hand on me, he's dead." She jerked on the binding that resembled a chain straitjacket built for two.

"So be it. If you kill him, then that only proves he isn't a man suited for the world we live in."

Nico's eyes widened. "But I'm not a man. I'm just a kid."

"Oh, *now* you're a kid?" Sindra scoffed. "In that case, if this kid touches me, I'm coming for *you*." She pointed at Dromon and then at the hooded man who'd taken her baby. Sindra flinched as they surrounded her, afraid someone would coldcock her again.

The chemist entered the room carrying the same needle that had sent Sindra into the heart of the Chasm. "No! No!" Sindra whipped her head back and forth, flailing, pulling Nico with her as she rolled on the floor.

The presbyters sat on her as the chemist administered the concoction into her arm. The walls, faces, and furniture kaleidoscoped into a blurry mess while her lungs searched for air.

"Now, she's not killing anyone." Dromon stepped aside as the room emptied, leaving only Sindra and Nico. "I'm sure you will have her complete cooperation. I will return in the morning."

The unity binding forced Nico and Sindra to face each other, their eyes locking unless they made constant effort to adjust their gaze. With this dose of drugs, some of her fear abated. She closed her eyes and forgot. Missing Myron, the loss of her baby, the discomfort of the binding all slipped away into a stream that trickled out of sight until she awoke.

• • •

She opened her eyes to see Nico staring at her, and her memory of the unity binding made her wish for the drugs to make her forget again. "Well, I suppose this marriage has been *consummated* by now." She was relieved that she'd gotten to sleep through being ravaged this time.

Nico lifted his head and tried to stand, pulling Sindra with him. "No." He avoided eye contact with her. "I—I couldn't do that—force myself on someone. And…even if I was of a mind to do such a thing—which I'm not—I don't know the first thing about consummating. You know? What goes where and when."

Sindra burst into laughter. "Now that's something new."

"Why are you laughing?"

"No reason." Sindra yawned. "How are we supposed to eat or take a squat in this thing?"

"Dromon'll come back and quiz us about last night. If we're official-like, they'll take this contraption off. If not, they'll leave it on until—"

"Just tell them we did it and be done with it."

Nico rubbed his forehead as though it hurt. "Didn't you listen to any of what I read to you from the holy books? Lying is an abomination. Except, according to the book of *Vogue* 1967, in the case of telling a woman she doesn't look fat in a dress or lying about whether the lobster bisque has no taste."

"And tying people together for a forced sexing isn't an abo—a bad thing?"

"Not between joined-up people."

"We are *not* joined up." Sindra gathered her hair and pinned it behind her ears. Nico's hands followed her moves, his knuckles hitting her in the face.

"Orkin joined us in the eyes of Judas and the Great Above."

"I don't care. Orkin is a baby stealer."

"Shut your mouth."

"Make me." They tumbled to the floor. Restrained by the unity harness, they could manage no more than a scuffle with straps and limbs getting tangled in the fracas. As they struggled to gain footing, their bodies slammed against the only shelf in the room, toppling a pair of wooden cups and a bowl to the ground.

The door unlocked. Dromon strolled in accompanied by three other presbyters. "Have you, in the eyes of the Great Above, made your union whole?" He glared at Nico, who bowed his head.

"No, sir, we have not."

Sindra shoved Nico.

Dromon turned on his heel, the way Rolf used to when he set out to investigate shittery on the salvage line. Pinky dropped a waterskin and followed the procession out of the room.

"Hey, what about food?" Sindra grabbed the water. Nico's hands rose to meet her face as she put it to her lips. Her hands then met Nico's face when he wrested the water from her mouth and took a swig himself.

"I have to drain." Nico squirmed in the binding.

"Don't you dare."

"But I can't help it."

They worked their way to their feet and made for the door, which was locked. The window, too, was locked. "We work together. Okay?" Sindra led them to the corner, to the squat hole in floor. "You go first. Then we'll turn around and I'll go."

"I can't go if someone's watching."

"I'll close my eyes. Okay? Just hurry."

As Nico squatted in the corner, the unity binding forced Sindra down with him. She heard the stream trickle to the baseboards.

They fell asleep hungry, sweating from the bulky harness that held them together, and they awoke to the sound of the lock clicking before the door flew open.

"Have you, in the eyes of the Great Above, made your union whole?" Dromon asked.

"Yes!" Sindra shouted. "For Chasm's sakes, yes. Get us out of this contraption."

Nico eyed Sindra. "No, sir, we have not."

Dromon exited with a frown, no food again, and this time no water, either.

With no food or water, they endured the stink of their own waste until they produced no more waste. Sindra had grown so sick of Nico's face that she fantasized about scraping it off with a draw knife like the ones she used in Jonesbridge to peel away rotten layers from a wooden recovery artifact.

When the door opened on the fourth day, and Nico held fast to his honesty in the face of thirsting to death, Dromon turned to the presbyters. "Orkin says to get this demon-possessed witch out of our village."

"Where?"

"What about Nico?" the other presbyter asked.

"Please don't banish me. I'll do what you ask—anything but this." He nodded to Sindra.

"Nico is very important to the future of our village. Since he is now married, he is of no use as a procreator. Get him out of the unity binding and send him to the reliquary shrine for ministry." Dromon motioned to the man in the hood.

Having had no food and scant water for the past four days, Sindra expended her remaining energy on drawing air into her lungs, leaving her with no more fight left to challenge the hooded man who'd stolen her baby. He bent down and began to work the combination on their right ankle first. After turning the mechanism back and forth, aligning tiny symbols on the lock, he gave it a yank. Sindra held her breath in anticipation of having one of the restraints removed, but the lock did not open.

"I can't open it." The hooded man's gritty voice grated on Sindra's nerves, as though he'd removed a layer of her skin with a paring knife when he spoke. He tried another, more accessible lock, this one on their right wrists. Again he shook his head. "It won't open."

"Of course it won't open." Orkin spoke from just outside the door. "The unity binding can only be removed with the Great Above guiding the hand. This sorceress has not sanctified this union. The Great Above does not smile on this marriage." He stepped into the room.

"Orkin." Dromon lowered his head in respect. Pinky and the presbyters followed Dromon's gesture.

"Give them water, along with a half dose. And take them to Carlisle."

"What does he mean, he can't open it?" Nico's voice shook.

"It means we have to breathe each other's hot breath until we piss ourselves to death." Sindra couldn't manage more than a mumble.

CHAPTER FOUR

Ahead of Myron, the hills and sky joined to form a wall of blue silhouettes, empty of water, its hand around the throat of what life remained. Behind him, the place he'd fought so hard to leave tugged at him to return where he could commiserate with the voices of other people and share in their struggles, lead them in their salvage efforts.

With the sounds of ghosts gone and the sky darkening, Myron finally stopped. He dropped Saul onto an embankment and collapsed, reaching for his waterskin.

"Water," Saul whispered. A pool of blood gathered beneath his head.

Myron sat up and rearranged the chain that connected him with Saul, inspecting the shackle for a weak point. The iron cuff around his ankle had a keyhole and a welded ring that held the link for the chain. Saul's cuff looked just as strong.

"Water." Saul's voice reminded Myron of the sound a cog makes grinding on a rotary sander.

Myron grabbed a rock and pounded at the shackle cuff. The limestone split in half. He scanned the ground for a more durable stone.

"Myron," Saul said, "I'm gonna die."

Myron jostled his waterskin, listening for water. He held it to Saul's lips, rationing out a drink, but, as he pulled it back, Saul reached for it and gulped down as much as he could. The struggle for the waterskin caused it to fall, spilling the rest of the water onto the parched soil, which sopped it up in a matter of seconds.

"People like you make me sick," Saul said. "Selfish to the end." He struggled to breathe. He put his hand behind his head, horrified to see it soaked with blood when he pulled it away.

Myron upended the skin over his own mouth and waited for one last drop to hit his tongue. "Backstabbing marks like *you* make *me* sick. Last thing I wanted to do was lug your sorry load halfway around Patriot's Pass." Myron banged on the chain with another rock. They each pulled their legs in opposite directions.

"I joined up to fight the E'sters the day I turned fourteen." Saul's voice shook. "They didn't make me fit for soldiering. Shipped me off to Jonesbridge—to do my part."

"The E'sters. The Alliance. What's the difference?"

"Sounds like something a traitor'd say."

"I'm not dying out here, Saul."

"If I'm dying, *you're* dying." Saul threw a sharp rock at Myron's head. Myron dodged, but the blood from Saul's hand splattered across Myron's face.

Saul held the back of his head with both hands. Blood oozed through his fingers. The dry earth soaked up the blood the way it had the water, leaving only a stain. His eyes telegraphed his panic, his resistance to accept the situation.

"We got to keep going." Myron began walking to the west.

Saul crawled in the opposite direction. Weakened by his injuries, he fell and rolled—anything to keep Myron from progressing. Myron removed his smock and knelt beside Saul. "We have to stop the bleeding." He tied his smock around Saul's head, a tight knot over the gaping wound in the back. Then he leaned back to rest. "We'll make it. Once we get to the ocean, we—"

"No…we won't." Saul sucked in a deep breath. His words sounded as though they originated at the bottom of a well. "We won't make it anywhere."

They sat at arm's length until the sun dipped below the hills and heat of the daytime in the desert gave way to cold air that bit at Myron's bare chest. His teeth chattering, his skin raw, Myron inched closer to Saul, hugging him for warmth. Saul protested with a grunt but did not open his eyes.

In Jonesbridge, Myron had grown accustomed to the absence of stars and moon in the smoke-filled night sky. Out here on the fringe of the Nethers, stars twinkled from one side of the frozen sky to the other, and the moon hung among them, in an upward crescent as if to catch the stars as they fell from the heavens. Myron imagined Sindra, wherever she was, holding the star he'd made for her, thinking of him. As the nighttime reached the peak of its dark and cold, Myron fell asleep to the mesmerizing chatter of Saul's teeth.

Dreams materialized. His grandfather was sifting

through the barn, searching for an undamaged steam piston for his barker wagon. His mother was still alive, calling them for a bowl of bone stew made with marrow, wild onions, and sour grinds. Myron kicked dirt clods through a wire hoop next to the barn, imagining where life would take him, where he might go, and what was left of the world to see. But this was a leftover dream he'd experienced before. It held no meaning except for nostalgia, a sentiment as restrictive as the shackle on his ankle.

When the sun hit his eyes, Myron jolted from sleep. Forgetting for a moment where he was, he stood up and walked in the first direction he faced until the tug of the shackle startled him. "Wake up, Saul. We have to find water."

Myron knelt and grabbed the chain with both hands, giving it a yank. "Come on." He noticed that the smock he'd tied around Saul's head was soaked with blood. He shook Saul. Saul did not awaken. Myron beat on the chain with a rock. He pried and pulled at the shackle. He could think of no possible way, with what he had at his disposal, to break free. Only one thing mattered now, and that was water.

Myron believed that he was a true slog, born of the Old Age experiment he'd discovered in the lab under the mountain. If his hunch was correct, that meant he could go without water longer than most people, but he had no idea how much longer. Several hours? A day? A few days? Myron hoisted Saul over his shoulder and walked in the opposite direction of Jonesbridge, toward the Great Western Ocean.

Saul's patchy hair tickled Myron's back, reminding him with every step that Saul had made the journey more difficult than it had to be.

He trudged along a ridge until his legs had weakened

too much to continue. He could tell by the sun that he'd traveled for hours, not minutes. His muscles ached and his throat cracked every time he tried to work up enough spit to swallow.

Myron put his hand just over Saul's mouth. No air in or out. His chest did not move. Myron had disliked Saul when he was alive; now that Saul had become a lifeless anchor, Myron despised him.

He searched for a heavy rock and struck Saul's leg just above the shackle cuff. Blood squirted out. He struck again and again, turning Saul's ankle into a purple mush, but he still could not get the cuff off or crush the ankle enough to get it from the shackle.

Myron removed Saul's smock and slipped it on. He worked off Saul's pants and put them on over his own, relieved to have some of the sun and wind blocked. With long strides, he hiked across the terrain, lifting his tethered leg, pulling it forward, yanking the chain with both hands with Saul dragging behind.

Ahead, a broken chain of jagged mountains flanked a basin so flat that it formed one wavy wall against the horizon. "Water!" Myron shouted. He collapsed into the lake, striking his head on the hard earth. He tried to splash his face. A fist full of salt flew into his eyes. No water, not a drop, only an endless salt flat populated with salt pillars. He turned back to the formidable landscape he'd just traversed. He pulled the chain. Saul's stiffening body inched forward.

He continued toward the west, a step, a pull of the chain, another step, hour after hour until a droplet of sweat rolled from his forehead. He jutted out his tongue, sipping the drop, trying to swallow.

"Gather 'round the kiln. Let your face feel the fire." Myron muttered the song before he started singing. "Your mama raised a fool if she taught you to dream…the only job to take for your family to feed…the steam shovel forty-five," he sang, his voice hoarse. "For the pennies and the pork, my life I will lose." He continued, now yelling the altered version of the Richterville funeral song, words the gravediggers in Richterville made up while sipping rot onion in the barrack yard. "Till my longing come home—Cincinnati steam shovel blues."

Myron's vision blurred. His arms outstretched, reaching for the sky, he continued humming the funeral song of Richterville.

• • •

"Hurry up. We have to get to town, Myron."

Myron's family rarely visited Richterville. His grandfather said that the townsfolk cast him a suspicious eye—because of the secrets he worked on in his barn. "Where is everybody going?"

"Sharma, the village doyen, has died. We must put her to rest," his grandfather replied.

At six, Myron knew of death from the lifeless soil and the spoiled sky, from the dead yards east of Richterville where gravediggers used a steam shovel to dig a hole wide enough to bury a hundred war dead at once, dusting them with lime before sealing them below the earth. But he had not yet seen anyone *put to rest.*

"Why does she need to rest if she's dead?" Myron asked.

"That's just an expression. The doyen was the eldest

person in Richterville—seventy-three long years in this inhospitable world."

"This is your first *passage*, Myron," his mother noted. "It is an important custom."

As they traveled along the road to Richterville, more people joined the procession, until a line of a hundred or more entered the village. A throng had already gathered, warming their hands around the brick kiln. The village center had a market on two sides, an infirmary on one side, and a masonry and coal depot on the other, forming a square where four paths converged. At its center, a gazebo topped with a clock tower chimed on the quarter hour, the only structure in Richterville as tall as the kiln smokestacks. The townsfolk called the back wall of the gazebo, covered in carved images, the story board.

A man wearing a robe climbed the gazebo steps and stood behind a podium. The crowd silenced as he patted down his thin wisps of gray hair. He scanned the faces around him and cleared his throat.

"I've known Sharma since we were both no more than knee high. I guess that makes *me* the oldest person in Richterville, now."

Myron noted the rare sight of smiling faces in the crowd, and a few chuckles.

"Death stalks us all. When it claims us, it chips off a hunk of our story and throws it in the garbage." His lip quivered as he adjusted his robe, a garment riddled with stains and holes that looked much older than any doyen. "And, as is our custom, the next in line for doyen," he said, patting himself on the chest, "must recount a tale from our past that speaks to the spirit of the bygone doyen." He gazed across the faces, and through the market, eyeing the jagged quarry at the bottom of the valley. His eyes misted. "Sharma and me used to sit in the field with the billet vine tickling our noses. Her grandmother—Lilly—some of you might remember her. She was the chemist in those days." He nodded toward a stand near the market that sold herbs and medicines. "She told us things while she gathered her witchworks in the hills."

Listening to the story, Myron wished he had someone his age to play with in a field.

The man went on to tell of times before the dry cracks in the ground widened into permanent channels. And he spoke of times before any rain that did fall left streaks of ochre in the dust. Before the squanderings and the culling when great beasts once roamed the world alongside people. And how the animals that did endure everything that the world had thrown at them were rounded up for gawkers on menagerie trains that traveled the surviving rail tracks between the Eastern Sea and the River Mississippi.

"Her eyes were hollow when she sat us down that day. She was our age, she told us, when the menagerie train whistle called her to the tracks. They stopped and set up a tent and erected a sign that read, 'Come see the spectacle of Carrie the Elephant!'"

He stopped speaking so he could wipe his eyes. When he continued, his voice tensed, shouting to the air as if angry with the sky. Myron's imagination ran with visions of the majestic and gentle creature the man described.

"She followed the signs. Bought her ticket. A menagerie roadie led her to Carrie's enclosure. There she saw the beast in the corner of a dark hole without enough room to escape her own waste. She was covered in flies and moaning. Lilly made me and Sharma pay close attention when she told us that she sat there all day with her hand on that animal's face as it wallowed and eventually died right before her eyes. Lilly said—without hesitation—that the Great Above called the very last elephant home that day."

The *elephant*, Myron noted, was one less creature in the diminishing dream of what he'd hoped he could discover out there in the world.

"This wasn't Sharma's story, but it was her grandmother's, and it's something we didn't talk about much after we heard it." He walked over to the story board. "Young folks are hard to come by these days. Babies aren't coming much into the world anymore, at least not around here. But we do have a few youths. Our youngest must now come to the stage."

Heads turned this way and that. Eyes hopped from face to face until the majority landed on Myron. His grandfather lifted on his tiptoes to see if he spotted anyone younger than Myron. "You're up. The youngest." He nudged Myron toward the gazebo.

"But—"

"Go on."

Myron walked through the crowd as it opened up for him to pass. He stepped up to join the man who was carving the shape of an elephant onto the story board. Myron fidgeted while the man finished, and then they walked together to the kiln firebox where Sharma lay on a plank, her eyes closed with slugs.

"Gather 'round the kiln. Let your face feel the fire," the crowd sang as they ambled toward the kiln. "The mornin' has broken. Stoke the funeral pyre." Myron stared at Sharma's corpse, wondering if she felt the burn all the way from the Great Above as her skin melted away in the kiln.

• • •

Myron gave the line between his leg and Saul's one last yank, urging his foot forward, until he collapsed in the middle of a salt flat. Cliffs with red and orange skirts grew no closer no matter how far he went. The only moisture left in his mouth was the blood that seeped through parched cracks in his lips. He lifted his waterskin above his mouth, waiting for a trickle or even a drop to find its way onto his tongue. When none came, he dropped his arm. He was a slog, but slogs, too, died from thirst, a slower and more painful process.

Myron closed his eyes and imagined himself and Sindra together on the beach in Bora Bora. The dream had evolved since he'd first concocted it. Instead of cerulean waves lapping at a pristine shore, Myron now saw a dried ocean with cracks the size of the Great Gorge and a beach paved by the skulls of ancient seabirds, Sindra asking him over and over how that place was any better than where they'd come from.

He smacked his lips, felt them touched by a damp cloth and a spray from the ocean that was not there. His mouth filled with water.

"Hey," a deep voice said.

Myron pried open his right eye to a vision of a man in the halo of the sun, leaning over him—Myron's custodian spirit here to escort him to the Great Above.

"Swallow if ya able." The man poured another mouthful of water into Myron's mouth.

Myron sat up to find three other figures casting shadows over him. They spoke slowly with a deliberate diction, but Myron couldn't make out the words. "Am I alive?" he asked, as his surroundings came into focus.

"Ye-ah."

The other people, a woman and two girls, continued speaking. "What are they saying? Why can't I understand them?" Myron tried to stand and fell back, having forgotten about the tether to Saul's leg. Saul's arms and legs splayed out spread-eagle behind him. Saul had taken a gray color and his limbs had gone rigid.

"They speakin' Gapi."

"Sounds like sleep talk."

"May as well be. Part Navajo, I think—a tongue as dead as that corpse you're dragging behind you. Old Age words from here and there. Some Mexican-speak. And a bunch of jabber you won't hear anywhere but out here."

The man pulled out a jagged knife and sawed at the shackle attached to Myron's ankle.

"Why don't you speak Gapi?"

"I do my best with it. But I speak like you, too, 'cause—" He reached for Myron's arm with a tight grip and placed the back of his hand beside Myron's. His eyes narrowed. "I been where you been." His hand bore the gear-and-hammer tattoo of Industry. "Name's Rounder."

The woman speaking Gapi held up her hand, shaking her head, trying to stop Rounder from freeing Myron from the shackle.

"What's wrong? What's she saying?"

"She says…it's a foul omen." He nodded to Saul. "You

being connected with a dead man like that. She says that if we free you, death will find someone else to attach to."

Rounder's face twisted as he hammered the shackle with a hatchet and pried at it with his knife. The woman looked on in dismay that Rounder had not heeded her warning. When he finally broke the chain, he flipped the broken end toward Saul and pounded on the hard ground. "Ground's too hard. Can't bury him here." He helped Myron to his feet.

Myron shook his leg. The cuff, still clamped around his ankle with three rings of a broken chain dangling from it, made a jingling noise when he moved.

"Used to, buzzards cleaned the messes we left behind. Now, guess we'll leave him for the wind and sand to clean his bones."

Rounder turned and picked up a satchel. They all plodded toward a contraption loaded with supplies, Rounder, the other woman, and the two girls, who turned every few seconds to look at Myron with a blank gaze. The girls were the same height. They had the same length of cropped black hair. Their faces matched pin for point and their mannerisms were identical. Myron could not tell one from the other. They were the same person, one on the left and one on the right, a mischief straight from the Chasm that left him feeling as though he might have died after all. They were also about the same age Myron was when the orange shirts killed his mother. "Which one is—the doppelgänger?" Myron asked, not wanting to go further until he reconciled the good from the evil.

"Huh?" Rounder turned toward Myron. "Oh, these here are *twins*," he said. "Nothin' to worry over. Came out the same is all."

The girls' mother admonished them in Gapi. The twins continued to stare at Myron. "What'd she say?" Myron asked.

"She tells them not to look upon the walking dead." Rounder smiled.

Hypnotized by the twins, certain that one must be malevolent and one virtuous, Myron found himself gazing back at them the way they stared at him. "What are their names?"

"Gapi names are peculiar. I call these two Rickets, 'cause of how sickly they look." Rounder continued toward the contraption. "I round folks up that are wandering the Nethers. Most people I come across already met with the same fate as your friend back there. Found these three in the belly of a rusted locomotive, buried half in sand, huddled over a man about to take his last breath."

The woman and her twins climbed onto a bench in the vehicle that resembled a mule-drawn wagon, but it had no mule, and, with four bulbous wheels, it looked as though it could traverse rugged terrain, unlike any wagon Myron had ever seen. As he approached the contraption, his interest piqued and his salvage instincts reached a boil. On the rear axle, he spotted a series of reduction gears driven by a sprocket that drove spliced-together bicycle chains.

Myron crawled under the front to inspect its inner workings. The front bench had two sets of pedals beneath a steering wheel at the end of a column that used a pinion to guide the wheels in the direction the steering wheel turned. Anchored to a metal plate under the chassis, a mast rose through the vehicle, towering above it with rope riggings.

"Where are we going?" Myron asked.

"Mesa Gap." Rounder pointed toward the west. "These

three I can take on in. You'll have to wait outside the gate until Te Yah reads your intentions."

"What about *their* intentions?" Myron asked of the twins.

"They look like they'd cut you from nut to nape if given the chance, don't they? Don't matter what their intentions are. I get water and supplies as payment for everyone I bring in. You have that Industry marking. Same as me. They don't trust it. I can't get past the gate either."

"Why?"

"Cause I won't undergo their fool intention ritual, that's why."

Rounder checked the ropes that tied down the water barrel and pouches of supplies, then checked the windsock that hung off the back. He licked a finger and held it into the air, motioning to Myron to sit next to him in the front seat. Rounder shouted something in Gapi and started pedaling.

The contraption eased to a start. He pulled a lever, and the gears ground as he pedaled faster. "Keep the pedals going." He nudged Myron, nodding toward Myron's feet, then he stood in his seat. A beam of wood at the base of the mast swung around as Rounder pulled a rope, and a sail rose into a giant triangle over the contraption. The sail filled with wind. The vehicle tipped to one side. Rounder strapped himself to the opposite side and leaned out to counterbalance the force of the wind, the vehicle's rotund wheels not deterred by any small defects in the otherwise smooth salt flat.

The speed of their travel invigorated Myron. It was as though they flew in an airship, but it was instead the next best thing—a landship. The cracked ground passed underneath them in patterns of yellow and white as the mountains grew closer.

"What is that?" Myron asked when he saw an obstruction in their path. It looked like a gathering of people in front of a machine.

Rounder furled the sail and hopped into the seat next to Myron, motioning him to stop pedaling. He pulled a brake lever and the contraption halted. From a compartment by the steering wheel, Rounder grabbed a telescope and extended it, squeezing one eye shut and peering through the lens with the other. "I don't know, but it can't be good."

CHAPTER FIVE

The unity binding made sitting, lying down, even scratching an exercise in contortionism and cooperation, but negotiating the swing bridges of Orkin's Landing turned into a painful and dangerous procedure. Sindra, the more agile of the two, stepped backward, while Nico traveled forward. Each of their arms connected in three places: bicep, forearm, and wrist. They grasped the handrails, coordinating movement—left, right, left—with each step. Nico whispered the rhythm for their movement across the bridge.

Both Sindra and Nico had been administered a half dose of the drug in the needle Sindra had received in previous days. This amount of medicine allowed them enough lucidity to walk, but it had put pillows on her feet and cool water on her hands, and made the flesh of Nico's face, inches from her own, resemble the scales on a fish and his eyes too far from his nose, a sight that made her laugh.

With each of Sindra's steps backward, Nico's step

forward became less in sync, until he lost his footing and slipped off the tightrope, hands falling off the hand lines, taking Sindra with him. Sindra landed on the rope they'd been walking on, Nico hanging in parallel beneath her by the fourteen restraints of the unity binding.

Sindra tried to stabilize herself. "Grab the rope."

"I'm..." His eyes closed.

"Nico! Wake up." Sindra wiggled until she got a grip on the ropes and arched her back to pull Nico up to the foot rope. "Nico!"

Nico's eyes eased open. He grabbed the rope and closed his eyes again.

"Come on." Sindra flailed around at random, causing Nico's body to respond like a marionette, rousing him enough to pull himself through the ropes. "We have to figure this out, Nico."

They continued the journey across the bridge, with Sindra having to wake Nico every few steps. Even at half of a dose, the medicine had a strong effect on his younger, smaller body. Dromon and the hooded man waited for them when they reached the other side. They spoke of scriptures and damnation, metals and locking mechanisms, and how Carlisle, the blacksmith, was not to know anything more than the basic facts.

Carlisle's house sat adjacent to the stables and the coal depot. She answered the door still dressed in sleep clothes. "What's the trouble?" She was a middle-aged woman, not quite Nico's height, with hair braided into tight rows that followed the contour of her head. Her hands, covered in burns and scars, brought to mind, in Sindra's imagination, the talons of a mythical bird.

"We need these pulled apart." Dromon pushed Nico and Sindra into the lamplight of Carlisle's house.

"Bring them into the forge." Carlisle grabbed a leather apron hanging by the door.

Sindra and Nico followed Dromon and Carlisle down a trail and sidestepped under an arch into a round building with a forge in the center. With a torch, Carlisle lit the sconces on the pillars in the blacksmith workshop. From her apron, she pulled out a pair of spectacles and positioned them on her nose. "Let's have an eyeball at this."

In the haze of medicine mind, Sindra watched the flames from the torches dance into vile creatures from the depths of the Chasm battling the torch for supremacy. They rose up with outstretched arms, withering, striking at the air with orange-tipped swords and the hearts of stars. The medicine had begun to soothe her instead of scare her.

Carlisle knelt down between Sindra and Nico. She examined the combination lock that connected their necks from one fitted metal collar to the other. "What the Chasm is this, Dromon?" Her eyes widened as she examined another of the fourteen combination locks that held them in parallel.

"It's a unity binding."

"A what?" Carlisle grabbed the chain that ran from upper arm to upper arm. She studied the cuff and the locking mechanism.

"A holy test—from Orkin."

"Where did *he* get it?"

"I don't know."

"Please just get us out of this thing." Sindra pulled on the binding.

"What do you need me for?" Carlisle put her hands on her hips. "Just unlock them and be on your way."

"The mechanisms will only unlock with guidance from the Great Above. It is a holy test."

"Do I look like the Great Above to you? How am I supposed to get them out of this contraption?"

"Pick the locks? Cut them out? I don't know. You're the metalsmith."

Carlisle rolled backward in a chair to a cabinet and dug out a set of picks and a magnifying glass attached to an adjustable stand. Positioning the magnifier over the most accessible lock, wrist to wrist, she studied the mechanics, moving the dials back and forth, working a random combination.

"Just cut them out and be done with it."

"Cut them out?" Carlisle smirked. "My best count, there are fourteen chains. One, two, three, four..." She began to count under her breath, the metal tinkling as her hand passed. "That makes twenty-eight cuffs to cut off of them. And if I heat this metal up enough to strike on the anvil, well—you may as well set these two kids on fire."

"Orkin thinks the girl's a witch."

"And what about poor Nico, here?"

"I wish I was a witch." Sindra glared at Dromon. "I'd cast the whole village into the sea."

Dromon slapped Sindra with the back of his hand. "Those chains aren't very thick. Cut them apart with a blade and worry with the cuffs later."

"There's another reason I can't cut it, Dromon." She focused the light from the magnifier stand onto the metal.

Carlisle wheeled back over to her workbench and returned with three saw blades. "These are the finest blades

I have." She led Nico and Sindra to an anvil. "Lean down." She pulled the slack from the neck chain and held it on the anvil. With Sindra's face on one side of the anvil and Nico's on the other, Carlisle's face sandwiched between them with the saw. After a moment, she reached for another blade.

"Where did Orkin get this contraption?" Carlisle groped for her last blade. With the magnifier over the spot she'd cut, she put her glasses back on and studied the chain. "Not a mark on it." She wheeled her chair until she slammed into Dromon's shins. "This is Old Age alloy. And these locks are Old Age ciphers."

"I don't know where he got it. He said that the Great Above had revealed a new stash of miracles, like when he found the books." Dromon stepped back from Carlisle with a worried expression. "In the lost city." He nodded toward the south, where remnants of a great city jutted from the ocean and hills like broken knife blades from a stump. "He said that the Great Above revealed a bevy of similar devices."

Carlisle's eyes met Sindra's and then Nico's. "So you put these two kids in this thing without knowing how to open it?"

"I am confident that the spirits would guide us if it is a holy union."

"I don't think this poor girl is any kind of a witch. And Nico's just a kid. This has to be one of the most diabolical devices I can imagine. I don't know how long you can live like that."

"Please, Miss Carlisle." Nico's eyes opened, not enough to see his irises, but enough to tell that he had not entered medicine sleep.

"Orkin says this girl is a witch and her presence has

already brought the village harm." Dromon gestured to the man in the hood standing in the shadowy perimeter and pointed a finger toward the west. "Take them down to the docks and get rid of them."

CHAPTER SIX

A plume of smoke rose from a smoldering wagon. Three men festooned in the regalia of painted bones placed a body atop the burning wagon. They paused, spotting Rounder's contraption approaching.

"Uh-oh. That there is the Votaries of Starick." Rounder retracted the telescope. He turned the steering wheel with such force that his cheeks reddened. "We gotta turn this thing around. Fast."

Myron knew of Starick, the custodian spirit of murderers. The vile, too, must be escorted, if not to the Great Above, then to the depths of the Chasm. Starick had the face of a raven on the slithering body of a snake. When a murderer died, Starick appeared over the body, reanimated it, and killed it again in the way that the murderer had killed his victims.

Myron and Rounder pedaled, but the contraption didn't accelerate enough to outrun their pursuers. As they grew near, the bones hanging from their tunics rattled with hollow *bonk*s. Myron saw the decorations on their faces and arms, fine designs drawn with the blood of their sacrifices.

"These nutcobs think that sacrificing folks'll pacify Starick. Keep him from paying them a visit when they die." Rounder reached under the seat and pulled a lever that released dozens of spiked obstacles behind the landship to slow down anyone, or anything, giving chase. "Ain't gonna be me," he said, out of breath from pedaling.

The woman on the back seat yelled phrases in Gapi, holding her twin daughters close to her side, as one of the men hopped onto the wagon bed. The front wheels tipped up and dropped back down. Rounder swerved, steering hard right and back left. The man lost his balance and tumbled off. Another reached for one of the twins' arms, got a firm grasp, and pulled. Her mother screamed and hauled her daughter back onto the seat, kicking the assailant in the head. On her other side, with both of the mother's hands occupied in the rescue of one twin, the third of the Votaries of Starick plucked the other twin from her seat.

Myron steadied himself, preparing to leap off the contraption to save the girl, but Rounder shook his head, slapping Myron back to his seat. "Keep pedaling or we're all dead." Two of the marauders pursued but ran out of breath as Rounder put everything he had into pedaling.

The woman stood, looking back at the dustup, yelling words from a language Myron didn't understand, but words he understood all the same—harsh condemnation, panic, paralyzed by the choice of rescuing one of her daughters or staying and protecting the remaining one.

"We can't just leave her," Myron yelled.

The remaining twin screamed next to her mother. She arched her back and writhed in the seat as if dying.

"What's wrong with *her?*" Myron asked.

"Scared, maybe?" Rounder asked the mom in Gapi if her daughter was injured.

The woman's voice shrill, her words shot from her mouth like arrows from a bow.

"She says the twins' bodies…" Rounder snapped his fingers, searching for the right word, "commiserate with one another. When one feels good, the other feels good." He swallowed hard. "When one's in pain—well, you get the idea. They've never been apart."

The lone twin's scream pierced through the jumble of sounds. She shook and rolled in the seat, kicking Myron in the back of the head. She fought to keep her legs together, and Myron imagined what her sister must be going through at that moment. It reminded him of the day the ghosts had violated Sindra, as he watched, trapped in the tunnel under the grate.

In her face, Myron could see Sindra's face, hear her screams, imagine her as a child. He scanned the stack of supplies for the hatchet Rounder had used to break the shackle chain. When he spotted it, Myron grabbed the hatchet and pulled the brake lever while Rounder still pedaled. "We can't leave her—not with *them.*"

"I always lose a few. To one thing or the other. Part of the job," Rounder shouted.

Myron hopped off the landship. The mom screamed, holding her remaining twin, urging Myron to save her other child. He shielded his eyes from the spray of dust that stirred up when Rounder began pedaling again. The Votaries of

Starick, surrounding the girl, stopped their violations and glared at Myron with crazed eyes.

Behind him, Rounder sped away. In front of him, he faced three maniacs armed with jagged pieces of metal. The captured twin writhed in the dirt, clutching her knees. Myron held the hatchet over his head.

The Votaries of Starick charged, shrieking angry bursts of Gapi.

Myron stood his ground, preparing to be run through with a sharp piece of scrap iron. The hatchet, a weapon that had left a mark on his family, would do so again if he could not wield it better than his mother had when the orange shirts came for Myron the day she died.

He dodged the first jab as the three arrived in a staggered line. His hatchet connected with bone, but not one that mattered—an unclean jawbone, still bearing sinew, hanging from the assailant's neck. As the three converged on him, Myron swung the hatchet back and forth, backing away. Behind the three marauders, he spotted the twin rushing with a length of wire they'd been using to bind her hands.

She leaped onto the back of one of the Votaries, looping the wire around his throat, and, with a hard pull, one that puckered her lips, she lessened their numbers by one. Myron tumbled to the ground, taking a blow with a metal rod across the back, losing his hatchet in the process.

Myron looked up to a welcome sight: an approaching dust cloud and Rounder's reddening face as he pedaled his contraption into the fray. Myron struggled to his feet and jumped out of the way.

When he saw the other votary run at the twin, aiming to

impale her, Rounder picked up speed, made a close pass, and smacked the attacker in the head with a pipe.

The other twin let go of her mother's hand and hopped out of the landship. She picked up the hatchet off the ground and lodged it into the back of the last remaining Votary of Starick. The twins joined hands, as though nothing had happened, and stared at Myron.

"Think their sacrifices worked to keep Starick from coming for them?" Myron wanted to stay and watch to see what, if anything, Starick would do with his fallen devotees.

"Chasm, no. If I thought that, I'd've tried it," Rounder said with a grin. "You don't really believe in all that custodian nonsense, do you?"

"I don't know."

"Hurry. We got to get off this flat before the sun goes down. Or them three maniacs'll be the least of our worries." Rounder adjusted the load on his landship. "Pull some crazy drack like that again and I ain't coming back for ya, hear?" When he removed the burlap tarp and repositioned the water barrels, Myron spotted several books protected under a board, but Rounder had them shielded from view.

Myron glanced at the twins again, clutched by their mother as though they had not killed with such ease moments earlier. Their eyes met Myron's, but he felt no connection to them. The mother had two fresh trails on her cheeks where a pair of tears had trickled through the dust and grime. She dug through a bag at her feet and pulled out a carved wooden flute and offered it to Myron. She held each of her daughters' hands and lifted them as if to thank Myron for what he'd done to save them.

Rounder scoffed and situated the hatchet next to

himself on the front bench. "Not takin' any chance with those two." He made a whistling sound as he shook his head at the twins. "Ain't going to sleep with them around."

Neither the twins nor their mother had said a word since the incident with the Votaries of Starick, while Myron and Rounder pedaled toward the setting sun. Myron studied the flute the twins' mother had given him. It bore intricate carvings and the markings of age, with indentations around the finger holes where use had worn away the finish. He put it to his lips and blew, producing a huff of wind with a soft whistle, then he shrugged and tucked it into his smock.

"I saw some books." Myron nodded toward the supplies in the back. "Where'd you get them?"

"Oh no, don't go asking questions about my stuff. I work hard for it. You hear?"

"It's just that I—I used to have some books."

"You know how to read?"

"Yeah."

"How'd *you* learn?"

"Grandfather," Myron said. "He was educated."

Rounder's gaze changed from stern to wistful. "The only reason I do this bit"—he gestured toward his passengers in the back—"is so I can find more stuff like that."

"Out here?"

Rounder motioned for Myron to pedal faster, pointing to the sun that had almost dropped behind the gray teeth of the distant mountain range. "Every time I come upon a jumble of Old Age ruins, I dig for books—pamphlets, signs, folders, anything. Maybe I could build a library, you see."

"Old Age books?"

"I'm guessing they are. I haven't learned reading yet. But

I will." Rounder shoved a wad of billet thistle into his mouth until his cheek poked out from his face. He offered some to Myron, who grabbed a pinch of the dried leaves from the outstretched pouch. He welcomed anything to dull the pain in his head from the past few hours.

"Why do you collect books if you can't read them?" He accidentally swallowed some of the billet thistle, which caused him to retch almost immediately over the side of the landship.

"What concern is it of yours? Don't matter to you what I do." He pointed a finger at Myron. "'Cept the fact that I saved your buzzard-food ass out there on the flat."

"Can I see your library? I can read the books for you and tell you what they say."

"Chasm, no. The only way I survived this long out here is not trusting no one."

Myron held the back of his hand out to remind Rounder of their kinship to the Industry Administration. "Can you at least help *me* find some books?"

Rounder's jaw clenched as he shook his head.

Up, down, around, Myron pedaled until his legs threatened to pop the way a rubber drive belt breaks when it gets too hot. The idea of a library, even one constructed by an illiterate Rounder, transformed the hostile landscape of the Nethers into a place of wonder. He gazed in all directions, imagining Old Age leftovers, structures and vehicles that harbored books with clues to the life the Old Agers led and why it all went away, why Myron had been cheated from the marvels of technology that they enjoyed.

She never said as much, but Myron had been sure that Sindra didn't believe a lot of what Myron claimed about the Old Age. They were as mysterious as the Great Above, the way they lived, the marks they left, and the way they had disappeared.

• • •

Myron and Sindra sat beside each other on the front pew of the chapel. Sindra stared at the steep side of Iron's Knob through the window as though the stained glass were still intact enough to divide the monochromatic landscape into a kaleidoscope of color. Myron tried to see what she saw, but his eyes wouldn't leave her face. She hadn't said much since he'd promised to take her with him to Bora Bora, except that she didn't want to be an extra burden on his flying machine.

"Once, when me and my grandfather were going to escape together," Myron lowered his head, "he told me a saying. That if you want to go quickly, go alone. If you want to go far, go together."

Sindra cocked her head. "Old Nickel said something like that too, out on the rails. The reason we were a *band* of railwalkers instead of a passel of lone walkabouts. 'Scatter to survive. Come together to live.'"

"Makes sense." Myron nodded. "We'll make it. It may take us years to reach Bora Bora, but—"

"And what if there isn't a Bora Bora?"

"We'll follow the tracks. Just like you did."

"The tracks? From one heap of broken shat to the other. I've been out there, Myron. There's nothing like what you describe." Sindra stood up and kicked a stone into the crumbling front wall of the chapel. "If the Old Age was so great, why isn't anything they built still working?"

"My grandfather said that, in the Old Age, they replaced all their books with machines. When the machines failed, everything went *poof*." He opened his fingers like an explosion. "But there are books still somewhere out there. My grandfather had some. When we get out of Jonesbridge, we'll find some. Most of them are fanciful stories, but you never know what they'll show us."

Sindra took Myron's hands. "I love that you're so full of hope. But getting out of Jonesbridge…I don't think that's possible."

• • •

Sindra's words haunted him as he recalled her flight into the clouds above the Gorge and how much preparation and time had gone into building the airship. It wasn't possible to escape Jonesbridge without a lot of know-how and a good deal of luck.

"How did *you* get out of Jonesbridge?" Myron asked, as he eyed Rounder's tattoo.

Rounder rubbed his neck with a sour look on his face. "That was a good ten, maybe twelve years ago, kid. Time doesn't really exist in the Nethers."

"But how?" Myron insisted.

"How'd *you* do it?"

"You saw me, shackled to a dead man."

The wheels of the contraption bobbled over rougher terrain as they left the flat behind them and entered the hills. Rounder bit his cheek. "One day, a few of them ghosts held me down and dropped a squat—right here," he pointed to his nose. "The smell of that ghost shat worked me into a hard boil. I ain't proud of what happened after that."

"But how—"

"Look, kid, motivation is sometimes its own reward." He held up his hand just as Myron's mouth opened. "Don't speak of it again."

As the orange hues of evening faded to purple, Rounder steered the landship between two rock formations and pulled the brake. He barked something in Gapi, and the twins and their mother climbed out of the landship. Myron followed. Rounder rotated a lever by the front bench, and both benches flattened to form a bed. He untied the sail and draped it over the contraption, where it fit snugly around the corners to form a tent. From the supplies, he reached for a metal can full of wax and lit the wick with a flint striker. Shadows from the flames rose up the triangles of fabric on all sides, following a tendril of smoke that wafted through the hole at the top.

Rounder held a cup under the water barrel spigot and turned the valve. A trickle of water filled the cup. He handed it first to the mother of the twins, then to the twins in order from left to right. He refilled it and handed the cup to Myron. The water stung Myron's throat when he threw his head back to get every drop in the cup.

After Rounder took his drink, he fished a hard loaf of bread from a burlap sack and broke it into fifths, handing everyone a share. With a flat spoon, he dug into a tin and wiped a smear of green gelatin on the bread rations, starting with the twins.

"This here is a bit of hoof pass and buckle mint."

Rounder continued adding the green mixture to the mother's bread and then to Myron's.

Myron sniffed the part of the bread covered in hoof pass. He withdrew by instinct when the odor hit his nose.

"It don't smell like much, but it'll give you the breath of a bull. You'll need it for pedaling over that god-forgotten Sad Mind range tomorrow."

Rounder gave instructions to the mother and twins in Gapi. He turned to Myron. "You're going to keep first watch. Keep a sharp eye for any movement out there—and watch them twins. No telling what they're up to." He snapped his fingers. "And if you have to squat or weddle, do it downwind from camp. The smell might attract…things."

"What kind of things?"

"I don't know." Rounder handed Myron a strip of sharpened rebar and lifted the fabric of the sail for him to step out.

The full moon illuminated the towering rock formations situated between the mesas on either side. The quiet struck Myron. No turbines spun, no wind blew, no one spoke, no coyotes howled, no bombs exploded, no orange shirts yelled, no overloaders released steam pressure. The crunch of his foot on the sand and sharp stones broke the silence, and Myron figured he could hear the snap of a shin pine branch if it happened twenty hects away. He sat down on a boulder that resembled a chair and waited for something to happen, for nothing to happen, for his turn to sleep.

Staring into the Nethers, a landscape as beautiful as it was dead, the rock formations mesmerized him. They alternated heights, taller to smaller, as if to march across the horizon. Myron pulled out the flute the twins' mother had given him.

He'd grown accustomed to the staccato melody of the pings and pangs of hammers on iron, what passed for music in Jonesbridge, but he loved the sound of a horn or the strum of a crate banger, the guitars people in Richterville created by cutting holes in wooden boxes and spanning them with taut strings.

He put the flute to his mouth and blew, covering the holes one by one with his fingers, producing a whistle no better than steam piston. He played until the cloth on the landship rippled, assuming it was Rounder coming to relieve him. Instead, one of the twins slipped under the fabric alone and sat beside Myron on the boulder.

She pointed a finger to her chest. "Gah-té," she said, patting herself. "Gah-té." She turned her back to Myron, lifting her shirt to reveal a jagged scar that ran the length of the left side of her torso.

"Gah-tah?" Myron gestured toward her.

"Gah-*té*." Her lips pressed into a flat line approximating a smile, giving him a nod. She reached out for the flute, placed it lengthwise on her palm, and turned it in the opposite direction, indicating that Myron had been blowing through the wrong end. "*Fauta*." She tapped the flute.

"Fah-tah," Myron repeated.

"Fah-*oo*-tah." Gah-té took Myron's hand and blew on his skin. "*Así*." A light stream of air hit his flesh as if she brushed it with a feather. She then blew as hard as Myron had been doing, so he could see the difference, and wagged her finger. "*Nop*."

Gah-té closed her eyes and put the flute to her lips. Her song began with a string of notes that persisted without hiccup or pause until the tune lulled Myron into visions of stars and flying, unaided by machines, with wings for arms. It conjured images of green fields of clover withering into a sea of dry stems beneath him. Her music transported him to a different time and place, not a better or bleaker place, but unfamiliar, and he didn't want it to stop.

As she finished her song, the flap on the landship flipped open again. The other twin joined them on the boulder. "Mah-ré." Gah-té pointed at her twin. Mah-ré turned her back to Myron and showed him her scar that ran the length of the right side of her torso, the opposite of Gah-té's.

Gah-té joined her hands together, nodding at her twin, and then ripped her hands apart. She repeated this action, this time pointing first at Mah-ré's scar. She joined her hands again, fingers interlocked, and pulled with a scowl on her face, her fingers holding onto one another until she wrenched them apart. She did this again and again, each time with her face more distressed until Myron finally made the leap that the twins had once been joined together, separated by a surgeon's knife. Though the thought of such a creature gave Myron a knot in his stomach.

"Mah-ré." Gah-té spoke her sister's name and swooned, acting as though she'd died, after which she spoke her own name and came to life. She gestured with her hands, repeating.

Myron's interpretation of her actions changed several times, but he finally surmised that *mah-ré* in Gapi meant death, and *gah-té* life, but he also thought it might have meant tired and energetic—or asleep and awake.

Mah-ré pointed at Myron, placing her finger on his chest. "*Haash yini*?"

"My name?"

"My name?" Mah-ré repeated.

"No. *Myron.* My name is Myron. My-ron."

Both Mah-ré and Gah-té spoke his name at the same time as they returned to the landship and settled beside their mother. Minutes later, Rounder relieved Myron of watch so he could sleep, but thoughts of Sindra kept him awake, the question that etched his soul. Was the wind sandblasting her bones clean somewhere in the Nethers?

When light struck the red and yellow mineral striations that skirted the rock formations, Rounder rousted Myron from half-sleep. He prepared the contraption for travel in a matter of minutes without saying a word. They made quick time in the morning as Myron and Rounder peddled toward Mesa Gap. Unlike the day before, when Rounder had been up for conversation, he didn't even acknowledge Myron's presence or his effort on the pedals.

The clack of the supplies on the wagon bed and the crunch of dried earth under the wheels were the only sounds until they arrived upon a paved trail, a wide, Old Age highway pocked with cracks and holes, washed out on one side. A battered road sign hanging from one post read:

BARSTOW 35
VICTORVILLE 67

The highway stretched all the way to the horizon in both directions, a marvel of Old Age engineering, but instead of heading southwest, continuing their journey to Mesa Gap, they turned up the highway in the other direction. The mother of the twins stood up. "Nop. Nop." She wagged her finger, shouting in Gapi as she urged her daughters off the moving landship.

Myron cut his eyes to Rounder for an explanation.

Rounder and the mother exchanged a few heated phrases, ending when the mother spat toward the northeast.

"She's cursing me for going the wrong way, but I've gotta get some supplies." Rounder dug through his stash, moving the water barrel and resituating the load before pulling out a shotgun. He broke it open where the stock met a pair of barrels, showing the empty barrels to Myron. "Don't want to travel this road without shells for my strong arm. And there's only one place I know to get them."

"We have to have them?"

Rounder swung the shotgun toward the southwest, toward Mesa Gap, and chuckled. "Never know what we'll find down *that* way. I sure as Chasm don't want to go without some insurance."

Gah-té left her mother's hand and approached Myron and Rounder. She pointed up the road opposite of Mesa Gap, toward the northeast. "Myron?"

Myron nodded. "Yeah, I'm going wherever Rounder's going." Having no knowledge of the terrain and no water, sticking with Rounder made the most sense.

Mah-ré pulled her mother toward the contraption to meet Gah-té. "Myron." She pointed northeast. "We… with…Myron."

"Listen to that. They'll be talking like us before long," Rounder said.

The twins and their mother climbed back onto the landship while Rounder wetted his finger and stuck it above his head. "Wind."

While Myron pedaled, Rounder unfurled the sail. The smooth pavement passed beneath them at a speed Myron had never experienced, except for the train that had brought him to Jonesbridge, but the train had no windows and no way to track the speed of the earth whizzing by. No matter how far they traveled over patches of potholes and gravel, the Old Age paved road never came to an end.

As they rounded a bend, a depot came into view on the horizon. Rounder lowered the sail and joined Myron on the pedals. After a moment, he held out his hand for Myron to stop. The landship creeped to a halt with the details of the depot still fuzzy in the distance. Rounder extended the telescope, closed one eye, and peered through the lens, mumbling to himself, what sounded like counting.

He collapsed the telescope and pedaled his contraption to within walking distance of the depot, which consisted of a storage barn, two sheds filled with coal, a cistern for water, three mules in a corral, a long barracks, and an adobe structure with a wooden door and windows. Coils of smoke billowed from the chimneys of two steam wagons parked behind the depot, fireboxes hot and ready for travel.

Rounder slipped on a pair of work gloves and instructed the twins and their mother to stay put. "Myron—*you* come with me."

Myron walked past the coal sheds lined up by the road. Bile rose up his throat. The coal and the smell of smoke reminded him of Jonesbridge, reminded him of his freedom, something he would have traded if it meant he and Sindra could be together again.

"Wait here." Rounder walked up to the door. He knocked twice, waited, and knocked again before opening the door.

Myron peeked into the window. Shadows moved up the wall inside the depot. Three sets of footsteps sounded on the floor, and he heard voices, one nothing more than a whisper.

The sounds struck him with familiarity, though he couldn't place them in his mind. Not until the door opened and two orange shirts stepped out did Myron place the sounds: ghost boot heels striking the floor.

Myron turned to run, but the ghost grabbed his arm and twisted it around to see the Industry tattoo. "You should've let them execute you in Jonesbridge. Death's too easy for you now."

"No—no!" Myron yelled. "I'm not going back."

Rounder refused to look at him as he counted the shotgun shells in the box he carried. "I'm sorry, Myron. This here ammo is too valuable."

Myron realized why Rounder had put on the gloves. Before he gave Rounder up for being an Industry fugitive too, Myron eyed the twins and their mother, knowing what the ghosts had done to Sindra, wondering what would happen to them if both he *and* Rounder wound up being captured. Myron bit his tongue to keep from speaking and vomited the last swig of water he had taken, along with a mouthful of stomach juice that burned his throat.

CHAPTER SEVEN

Sindra and Nico sat face to face in the cargo hold of a boat, still joined in the unity binding. The smells of ocean water were new to Sindra, having lived her entire life in the dust, but the stale air in the boat's hold smelled of sweat and urine, scents she and Nico had brought on board themselves.

She made out three distinct voices on the deck above, one woman and two men, but the wood between the two decks smothered the specifics of their conversation, except for the cursing that came clearly to her ears.

"Any idea where they're taking us?"

Nico tugged at the binding chains. "No."

"None?"

"Wherever it is—"

"Why couldn't you lie? One time." She wasn't sure if she believed that the Great Above would have guided Dromon's hand or not. Nothing they might have done or told them they'd done would have helped them out of the impossible puzzle of a device.

"I don't know. I just couldn't." He fidgeted with the bindings. "I didn't want them to think…that I'd forced myself on you. It's wrong. I woulda felt guilty about lying—and about someone thinking I copped you while you were in medicine sleep."

Sindra allowed his comment to sink in, consider what it meant, and realized that it sounded like something Myron might have said, making her suddenly miss Myron more than ever. He always treated her with respect, not only as a woman, but as a person.

• • •

Sindra watched Myron explore the front of the chapel where remnants of an altar remained.

"Maybe we could marry up. Right here." Myron blushed. "I can build a preacherman with those boards over there. And here's his hat." Myron plucked a curved clay shingle off the ground.

"Why would you want to marry up with a carpie?"

Myron shoved the rotting altar over. It tumbled, splintering into two pieces. "You are *not* a carpie."

"Not by choice." Sindra stared at Myron's postcard of Bora Bora. "Does anyone ever choose to be a carpie?"

"You're Industry. Like me. A salvager, and a damn good one."

"I am."

"They steal your affections. And you can never let what someone steals from you describe who you are. Only what you give." Myron sat beside her on the pew. "If I give you me, and you give me you, what someone stole should never matter."

"You really don't see me any different? Being ravaged by ghosts and admins whenever they like."

"Yeah, I do see you different. As a survivor that kicks sand in their faces."

• • •

If not for Myron that day, Sindra questioned whether she would have spiraled into accepting her role in life as a carpie. The Orkinites had stolen her baby the same way the ghosts had stolen her body, and Myron had been right—she could choose to become a victim of theft, or choose to be a survivor of it.

"Thanks, Nico. You know, for not—you're a nice kid. But nice people get carved into trophies out here."

"I have to get out of this thing." Nico squirmed as tears rolled down his cheeks. "I can't take it anymore. Trapped like this." He struggled to pull one of the restraints over his shoulder.

Nico jerked his arm, yanking Sindra's with it. Sindra yanked back, and after a pop, Nico screamed. "My shoulder!" His arm dangled from his shoulder. "My arm came out of its socket."

He coughed and moaned. They both wiggled, turning their heads in opposite directions to avoid breathing each other's air. Nico sobbed as his arm hung loose. Sindra grasped his bicep with one hand and the top of his shoulder with the other. She strained, pushed, and groaned, until finally she gripped his arm with both hands and rammed him into the wall shoulder-first, popping the joint back in place. He gritted his teeth and groaned.

With Nico in such pain, Sindra thought of the drugs the Orkinites had pumped into her arm. It had battered her mind into submission, and then it welcomed her home with a soft bed, warm and inviting, every point on her body alive and dead at the same time, worries and strife no more than a breeze over her chest. The moment she returned from its influences, she longed for it again, and that longing had become an ache.

"What was that stuff they gave me? In that needle."

"It's called Mercy." Nico's voice trembled.

"What's in it?"

"Why?"

"Maybe we can make some ourselves."

Nico wiped the tears from his eyes. "I don't know. Last year, when I was assigned chemist apprentice, I saw what went in it. That was before the chemist ran me off in favor of Joam." He shook his head. "Anyway, trust me, you don't want to make that."

"Maybe. Tell me what's in it!"

"It's hard to make."

"I don't care." Sindra stomped her foot on the deck.

"All I know is that it has three main ingredients. There's a fungus called beast's breath. It grows in the caves by the village. It gives you spiritual visions. The main thing is the juice from a poppy flower, really hard to find. Grows in the Nethers." He nodded to the east. "Also, there is artemisia. It's all cooked in solution. I know what's in it, but I couldn't make it. If you do it wrong—" he pulled his finger across his throat. "It's bad stuff. They only give it to people on the edge of death. That's why it's called mercy."

"I wasn't almost dead."

Nico squinted, staring up in a thinking posture. "I guess they use it to convert nonbelievers, too." He and Sindra leaned against the wall. "Sometimes a heretic will denounce the path. Orkin'll give them Mercy and minister to him to correct his ways. So, I guess almost dead, physical-wise—and almost dead, soul-wise."

The boat creaked as it changed course, producing a sound that reminded Sindra of a baby's cry. "How do I get her back?"

"Your baby?"

"Yes." Sindra swiped Nico on the side of the head. "Who else?"

"You can't."

"I will."

"Impossible."

Sindra smacked the other side of his head. "Stop talking stupid and think." Nico did have much in common with Myron, but Myron would have already formulated an idea, even an impossible one.

"Orkin has his own island. No one except the presbyters and the Orkin's Landing Navy knows where it is."

"Navy?"

"Yeah. Sort of like a sea army on ships."

"I know what a navy is." If she'd had anything but bile in her stomach, she would have vomited at the thought of her baby out there on some island with a crazed preacherman and his navy. Instead, she heaved a dry burn up her throat.

"What's easier: make Mercy, or get my baby back? It has to be one or the other."

"Can't do either. Just knowing where to find the poppy flower, which I don't, ain't enough. You have to get to it. In the middle of the Nethers." He lowered his head. "And, unless you have your own navy—or an army, your baby—"

"I get it. We're headed for the dead yard with the wind at our backs." It gave Sindra solace to quote Old Nickel when things got rough.

"What are they doing up there?" Nico eyed the ceiling where footsteps, back and forth on the deck above them, echoed through the cargo hold.

A harsh voice yelled from somewhere off the boat. The footsteps grew closer, sounding from the stairs. A shirtless man with a chest full of scars bent down to clear the low passage, taking Nico and Sindra by surprise. He grabbed Nico by the arm. "Up. Let's go."

"I don't want to die."

"Me either."

Sindra saw the pain in Nico's face, the effort he put into hiding what might be perceived as a weakness.

"Please don't let them kill me, Sindra." Nico grabbed her hand.

"Whatever happens at the top of those stairs, we're in it together."

The boat docked at a pier that jutted halfway into a river full of yellow muck. The stink of the water burned Sindra's throat as she took a breath. A deckhand threw a rope, caught by a woman who wrapped it around a mooring post on the pier, while the other deckhand positioned a gangplank for boarding.

Sindra rubbed her eyes, wondering whether the Mercy had dulled her senses, when a man stepped on board, led by protruding belly that resembled a bag packed full of millet. His face drooped around his mouth under the weight of his jowls. The rations required for such excess flesh tested Sindra's imagination.

"What is this?" The large man grabbed the unity binding and tugged it as though he could remove it like a shirt, pulling Nico and Sindra together right up to the man's belly.

"We couldn't get it off," the boat captain said. "Even tried the hull cutter."

"Lorin won't want the kid." The large man tested the bindings again, pulling at the canvas fabric. "That's chain under there."

"Yeah, chains with combo locks." The captain took a knife and sawed the canvas to reveal the metal underneath. "Need a gas torch. Maybe steam hammer'd do the job."

"Just break the kid out of there and bring me the girl."

"Done told ya. Can't do it."

"You can if you chop that little rat into a hundred pieces."

"What?" Nico moved into Sindra, hugging her. "Please, Sindra. Don't let them kill me." Nico fell somewhere between choking and coughing.

Sindra studied the man who had suggested dicing up Nico to separate them. He wore no shirt, but dangling from his ear she spotted an earring with the symbol of Rok, a one-winged bird, the custodian spirit of prisoners. An old man on the rails had once told her that when someone who was once in prison for a crime dies, Rok determines whether they should return to prison in spirit or whether they had turned to a better life and can go to the Great Above.

"You sure you want to do that?" Sindra gulped. "Cut him up like that?"

"Whatever it takes."

"We two are a married-up pair." She nudged Nico. "Sanctioned by the Great Above. If you were hoping to maybe find a spot up there someday, might want to think again. Chopping folks to pieces doesn't sit well with the almighty." Sindra did her best impersonation of some of the more pious people she'd heard in Orkin's Landing.

The man rubbed his jaw where a patch of spindly hairs curled under his chin. His eyes narrowed as he pulled the binding again with a laugh. "I ain't really gonna chop this kid up, you dim fool. That'd leave a piss of a mess on this man's boat." His laughter caused his belly to shake. "And I don't fall for that custodian spirit hokus pokery, neither. Show me this Great Above and I'd think about choppin' him up, too." He shoved Sindra in the back to get them going. "That don't mean I ain't gonna kill this kid first chance I get. I prefer a cleaner process. Maybe toss him off that cliff to see how far I can hurl him." His laughter continued as he prodded Sindra. "But Lorin can do what he wants to him. Ain't my problem. Load 'em up."

They led Sindra and Nico across the gangplank to a steam wagon loaded with ore. "What's going to happen to us?" Nico whispered.

"We have to escape." She kept her response under her breath, so quiet that Nico did not hear it.

"Sindra?"

CHAPTER EIGHT

"A friend? Well, that's not an easy question." Myron's grandfather handed him a wrench to hold while he tapped a gear into place on the generator.

"These kids." Myron pointed to a page in an Old Age book. "They kept each other's secrets. But one of them told someone else the secret—and they're *still* friends."

"Keep reading. It's not all sorted out yet, I'll bet." Myron's grandfather held his hand out for the wrench.

"That's as far as I can read." Myron showed his grandfather the charred remains of the last half of the book.

"Well..." He rubbed the back of his neck. "Trust. That's the thing with friends—when you boil it down. But there's risk in friendship."

"Do you have any friends?"

"You're the only person I trust." He gave Myron a nod. "Having friends outside of family, well...that's sort of a luxury of a bygone era."

"What about Mom?"

His grandfather wedged a moment of reflection into the conversation. "Of course." He lowered his head. "I trusted her completely. But—her decision to fight that day..." He returned to his work, tightening a nut on the casing of what he'd hoped would produce electric power from pedaling on a stationary bicycle in the barn. "Sometimes, a friend does what must be done. It's not as easy as weighing slugs on a scale."

His grandfather defined a friend as someone with common interests, somebody other than family to spend time with, a person to confide in and lean on in times of trouble, someone to trust with the important details of life. Myron had no friends, except his grandfather, and had no acquaintances his own age, though he'd seen other kids in Richterville.

The Old Age books made friendship sound as though life without a friend was diminished, that a victory in life didn't mean anything unless there was someone to celebrate it with, and a defeat could only be survived with the solace of a friend. In the book he'd been reading, two friends, a boy and a girl, ten years old, a year older than Myron, came home every day after school, grabbed a pair of shovels from the tool shed, and dug a hole together, aiming to dig all the way to China. As they dug, they talked about what sorts of places they wanted to visit, what kind of vocation to aspire to, and, as the hole grew deeper and wider, and the days longer, their conversations turned toward secrets.

"You can't tell anyone. Promise?" she said. A shovelful of soil slid down the growing mound outside the hole. Reading this part had intrigued Myron. The boy promised, so they conducted

a ritual where they each cut their pinky fingers with a pocketknife and entwined them together, allowing their blood to mix.

Then the girl confessed that her father had done things to her that confused and scared her, and, when she'd told her mother, her mother had beaten her with a sharpening strap. Afraid for her safety, the boy told his mom what the girl had told him, but the two friends just kept digging the hole and the pages ran out just before the boy spilled his secrets.

• • •

Myron had kept a sharp eye out for a friend his entire life, never finding one until he met Sindra. Coyote Man had betrayed him. And Rounder, a kindred spirit, collector of books, Industry comrade, had sold Myron out for a handful of shotgun shells. He'd thought, or wanted to think, that Rounder could have been someone he could dig a hole with.

Trust, his grandfather had claimed, provided the foundation for any friendship, but Myron had never figured out the word, what it meant, without removing the human element. He trusted the strength of shackle that now bound his legs together. He tested it, yanked it, banged on it, as he had the one that had held him to Saul, the remnants of which still hugged his left calf above the new shackle. He trusted that the day followed the night, even in Jonesbridge, where the sun hid behind the smoke, but people proved less predictable, making his memories of Jonesbridge bubble back to the surface as quickly as his freedom had submerged them.

Chained to a support beam, Myron slumped in the

corner of the depot while two cockrels, what Netherides called Jonesbridge ghosts, sat across from each other at a table, gnawing on salted pork strap.

When Myron adjusted the heavy chain so that he could sit, the ghost closest to the door chucked a wooden block, used to keep the window propped open, at Myron's head. "Quiet over there."

The corner of the wooden block struck Myron in the forehead. He squinted as the pain shot down to his eyes.

"Soon as the afternoon patrol gets back—oh, in about half a click," he glanced out the window, "we're heading for Jonesbridge." The ghost pushed his chair back and stood up, glaring at Myron. The ghost went outside to check for signs of the incoming Civility patrol.

The other ghost knelt beside Myron. "I remember you," he whispered. "I'll do what I can to help you. Won't be easy." He stood suddenly when the door opened and his partner returned.

"Wind howling up a cordbuster out there." The ghost eyed Myron. "Here's hoping they find a new water hole." He tossed back a swig of rot onion. His face twisted as the burn hit his throat. "Got to bring some kind of good news back to Jonesbridge—besides this derelict slog."

Hearing the word sent a shiver down Myron's back. *Jonesbridge.* The salvage factory took shape in his mind, the rows of work benches manned by solemn faces, foremen pacing the floor, the clank of twisted metal, the smell of the furnace, the boom of a heavy crate of recovered war debris.

The door flew open. *Boom*, Jonesbridge disappeared. The ghost by the window fell across the table. *Boom*, the other ghost flew back against the wall, the orange fibers from his shirt blasted like a holiday confetti bomb. Myron's ears felt as though he were underwater. Blood dripped from the table into a red pool on the floor. Rounder stood with the shotgun, a shell between his teeth, reloading.

"Don't look so surprised." Rounder kicked the chair out from under the slumping ghost. "I wasn't going to leave you with these cockrels. I just needed two things." He grabbed the key hanging from a ring on the ghost's belt. "Some shotgun shells to fight them with, and the combination to their safe." He laughed. "They gave me both." He tossed Myron the shackle key.

Shocked by the noise, the blood, and the sudden change in outlook from free to imprisoned to free again had left Myron reeling. He couldn't move.

"Well, come on. When that patrol gets back," Rounder pointed to the barracks on the other side of the corral, "there'll be twenty or more of these beak-suckin' foggers looking to dice into bits whoever's responsible for this." He twisted the knob on the safe, stopped, rotated it again, and stopped.

The safe door creaked open. "Jackpot." From the safe, Rounder slid a dozen shotgun shells into a burlap bag, throwing in ten sticks of mining ordnance and a metal canister with a conical top closed with a cotter pin. "Get moving." Rounder slapped Myron across the side of the head. Myron's eardrums throbbed. Rounder lifted the slumping ghost's hand on the table and bit off a chunk of the half-eaten strip of salt pork.

Myron stumbled by the table. The sight of puddles of blood soaking into the dry wood turned his stomach.

"Why—you didn't have to kill them." Myron struggled

to breathe. He lifted the face of the ghost who'd whispered promises of escape. "He was gonna help me." Myron shoved Rounder in the chest.

"You're as dumb as you look if you think these folks help anyone but themselves." Rounder cocked his shotgun. "If that's the best *thank you for saving my sorry life* I'm going to get, I should leave you here chained to that post and let the ghost patrol have you."

Myron shoved his forearm into Rounder's throat, pinning him against the wall. "You left me with them in the first place." He pressed harder until Rounder gagged, until his face turned red and his eyes bulged. "Here's your thanks." Myron eased up on the pressure to Rounder's neck.

Rounder coughed and shoved clear of Myron, dismissing his display of indignation. "If you aim to stay out of Jonesbridge, you might have to do some killin'. These orange-shirted monsters extend their reach farther west every day." Rounder rubbed his throat and swallowed. "We don't stop 'em and we'll all be headed right back to Jonesbridge in a god-forgotten windowless train car—and the death odor of some poor slog in the dark corner." He struck the table with the stock of his shotgun.

Do some killing? Myron often returned in his mind to the Old Age textbooks with word problems for learning math that his grandfather showed him, and, in this way, he framed his confusion into a potential solution, if only to pacify the screaming questions. People killed, it seemed, in far greater numbers than they reproduced—the war with the E'sters, the battles for water, lunatics worshipping the custodian of murder. They ran from each other and either lived free and alone or with others in captivity. At what tipping point, he wondered, would there no longer be any new people to replace the ones who'd died? And slogs couldn't bear children at all anymore who didn't come out wrong, destined for death. The killing would have to stop soon.

"I've killed before." Even then, Myron hadn't intended to kill, just to stop the ghosts that were raping Sindra.

"My guess is these orange shirts are up to something." Rounder's voice trailed as he turned the corner. "They've been out here where they never used to be. Searching. For what? I ain't sure, but I aim to stop them here."

Behind the depot, Rounder took his hatchet to the water cistern supports until they gave way, toppling the cylinder and spilling enough water to quench the thirst for a year. With his hatchet, he scooped some fiery coals from the firebox of one of the nearby steam wagons . He jogged to the barracks and situated the coals so that fire crawled up the building, consuming the dry wood. He did the same thing to the coal shacks before he opened the corral and scared the mules into the desert.

"They'll die out there without water." Myron chased after one of the mules. The mules brayed, circling back into the corral near the burning depot.

Rounder pointed to a wall of brown haze on the horizon. "We got to get ahead of that sandstorm." He extinguished the fires from the steam wagons so the orange shirts couldn't follow. When he reached the landship, he gave Myron the signal to pedal and they sped onto the Old Age highway, glancing back at the mother and her twins and the curtain of sand hanging in the sky behind them.

Myron rubbed his ankle where the original shackle still pinched his flesh. They traveled in silence until the sun set, forcing them to camp under a washed-out bridge that cut the highway in half. At first light, they left the Old Age paved roadway for a dirt road, a deviation that Rounder claimed would cut a day off of their travel time.

Near midday, they crested a dune with a clear view of a settlement nestled in the protection of a butte. "Megan's Point." Rounder nodded toward the large collection of structures, the closest thing to a thriving town Myron had ever seen. "Thing about this place is, civilization hinges on mystery. No one knows what firepower I got under my tarp, and I don't know what they got. Megan's drudgers keep order. Watch yourself. They'll send us all to the Chasm in a breath."

"They have lights." Myron stared at the strings of twinkling bulbs stretched across the market alley.

"Don't be taken in by all the carousing down there. There's an old woman with a market stall that sells sweet confections, called doughnuts. And that's the *only* reason we're going. In and out. Hear?"

"Doughnuts?"

"Like chewin' on edible gold." Rounder returned to pedaling. "Got some slick to trade in, too."

The Netherides referred to *water* as a canteen-ready consumable. *Slick* described a fluid that could be consumed only after a copious amount of filtration and preparation, which included any liquid that fell from the sky and some that flowed on the ground. Slick fell between water and slime, good for steam boilers, as it wouldn't produce toxic steam like slime. Slime held no value, except in Mesa Gap where Rounder claimed they could process it with a sort of Old Age magic.

Megan, Rounder explained, was one of a dozen or so Netheride nobles who ruled their own little fiefdoms in the Nethers. Megan controlled a water filtration apparatus that turned slick into water, for a price ratio of one gallon of slick to one pint of water, an eight to one rip-off, according to Rounder.

Heat waves on the road looked like puddles of disappearing slick as Myron and Rounder pedaled toward the town gate, which was protected by clusters of wooden spikes, rolls of razor wire, and broken bottles wedged into stacks of rubber tires. The town gate stood open and unguarded, except for the lookout in a turret constructed above the façade of an Old Age storefront bearing a faded sign that read DISCOUNT TIRE.

A severed head, week-old, shriveled in the sun, dangled from a rope tied through the eye socket. Beneath it hung a sign with a symbol scrawled in blood. "What happened to that guy?" A pang of dread greeted Myron as they rolled past the gate.

"Gapi don't have written words. Just pictures. That there is the symbol for thief."

The mast of Rounder's landship banged the DISCOUNT TIRE sign as they entered town, tilting the landship until they corrected course.

"Megan's a merchant sort of woman. Commerce and the like. You might get away with killin' someone around here, but stealing…" Rounder nodded to the severed head. "Stealing don't work in a place built for buyin' and sellin'. And Megan, she'll sell anything for the right price."

Rounder parked near a bandstand in the town center, where three windmill generators pierced a hole in the market alleyways covered in low-hanging fabrics and planks to shield the sun. A dozen people on the bandstand banged on barrels and drums, plucked cables, and danced with tambourines.

A drudger approached the landship and marked it with a coal stick, then made the same mark on Rounder's arm, temporary parking. If they stayed so long that the symbol on Rounder's arm, from sweat or heat or crowd, no longer resembled the one on the landship so that Rounder could claim it, Megan would have the ship hauled away to the auction pit.

The structures in Megan's Point huddled with one another in a dense jumble, shanties on top of stalls, in, around, and on top of Old Age rubble, mixing the old world with the new in an architectural stew. Aside from the three windmill generators, the tallest buildings, situated just above the fray, were the guard houses where drudgers eyed the goings-on to keep order.

One of the guards' eyes stayed fixed on Myron. "Why's he eyeballing me like that?"

"Probably looking at them twins behind you." Mah-ré and Gah-té stood between Myron and their mother.

"*Dosh łé'étsoh.*" Rounder held up two fingers and stepped up to a counter in a shadowy alcove. He dug through his bag and slapped down a chunk of copper ore.

A woman lifted off her stool and inspected the rock before wagging her finger at Rounder. "Nop."

He fished a thin tab of refined copper from his bag and held it up.

The woman nodded and pulled two wooden cups encrusted with white chalk from under the counter. She filled each one halfway from a spigot under a barrel.

Rounder reached for the cups as she pushed them forward. "Rat wine. Don't know what the Chasm it is, but it takes the edge off." He handed one of the cups to Myron.

The mother of the twins smacked Rounder in the back of the head and shrugged, as if she'd expected a cup as well. Myron gave her his, and Rounder held up another finger with a sigh, and then three fingers when the twins' mother made it clear through an insistent gesture that the twins would also partake of the rat wine.

Rounder snapped a Gapi phrase at the twins' mother before turning to Myron. "I didn't take these girls to raise." He held his cup to his lips. "Might help to hold your nose." Rounder squeezed his nostrils and tossed his head back, swallowing hard with a grimace.

The rat wine felt like chewing on a hunk of white-hot coal, something Myron had never done, but his imagination filled in the blanks as the fiery sensation mixed with unexpected chunks of a chalky substance, some that slithered down his throat. The bit he couldn't bring himself to swallow sat under his tongue while his eyes watered and a bead of sweat rolled down his jaw.

"Don't let it linger too long." Rounder patted Myron on the back.

The rest of the rat wine slid down Myron's throat. When he finally opened his eyes, the colors of the market exploded with green and yellow, and, as he followed Rounder to the stall around the corner, the faces in the crowd mingled, forming an image like the one in the kaleidoscope his grandfather had made for him.

"Jasper." An old woman left her stall to give Rounder a hug.

"Hi, Ktala." He glanced at Myron. "But it's Rounder now."

"I've known Jasper since he was no higher than a shin pine," Ktala said to Myron. She turned to speak to the twins' mother in Gapi, and they both laughed. Rounder's face turned red.

"I know why you're here. Sure as Chasm ain't to see your old Auntie Ktala." She ambled into her stall and returned with a single disc of fried dough, covered in a glaze, with a hole in the middle. "Ain't had no shipments of confectioner powders going on, oh, ten days."

Ktala pulled apart the doughnut and offered one half to Mah-ré and the other to Gah-té. "Made the last batch this morning. Only one left, I'm afraid." She wagged her finger at Rounder as he watched the girls bite into their treat, staring at them as though they were gnawing on his own flesh. "You wouldn't deprive these two what you got at their age, would you?"

Gah-té, with one bite left, nudged it toward Myron. He took the morsel and popped it into his mouth. "How do you say thanks in Gapi?"

"What does it matter?" As Rounder walked away, Mah-ré gave her last bite to him. He sighed and shook his head. "It's *ahéhee*. Thank you."

"*Ahéhee*," Myron said.

Where the rat wine had burned, the doughnut dissolved on his tongue in waves of joy.

"We best get going. Can't get stuck here. Gates close at night and this place turns into an entertainment for those with sickness of the mind. We need to get out of here. Now."

Rounder navigated the growing crowd at the town center, trying to get back to his landship. With the symbol on his arm still fresh, the drudger let him pass. Myron led the twins through a crush of onlookers pushing toward the bandstand.

With Rounder's landship now stuck, surrounded by people, Myron stood up on a bench for a better look at the crowd gathered at the edge of the platform. A boy, weathered and weary, whose bones wore his skin the way smock hooks hung burlap, stood as if to lean on an invisible wall behind him. A man in a leather apron pointed. "Here we have what looks to be a healthy boy, ten or so. Make a strong workhand. In a few years, might even be able to help some of you road hags bear a child. Bidding starts at three gallons of slick."

A man looked at the woman standing beside him and raised his index finger when the auctioneer rattled off his call.

"What's going on?" Myron stretched for a better look.

"Looks like a slave auction." Rounder stepped down off the wagon and untied the rope that held his supplies to the landship.

"People? Sold on the block? That's not right."

"Maybe it ain't right, but it'd take more bullets than what I got to alter the natural order of things."

"Where'd that kid come from?"

"Who knows? People roam the Nethers searching for something. Most of them aren't sure what they're looking for—or if they'd know it if they found it."

Myron understood. He wasn't certain he would know it if he found Bora Bora. How could he differentiate one island from another?

"One of three things happens to roamers out here." Rounder pulled out a brown bag filled with prairie bread and shoved a wad into his mouth. "They curl up into a clump of dried flesh and croak." Crumbs flew from his mouth as he spoke. "Somebody like that fat jack up there finds them and sells them to the highest bidder. Or, if I find them first, they wind up in Mesa Gap, provided they're Gapi, *or* Te Yah reads their intentions to be honorable." He bit off another chunk of bread. "And that's it." He cocked his head and turned back to Myron. "Until now. With orange shirts pushing west, I guess a poor soul is about as likely to wind up in Jonesbridge as anywhere these days."

The highest bidder, one of only three interested parties in the crowd of fifty, ended up paying three gallons of slick, a half-crate of coal, a strongbox, and length of rope for the boy on the platform.

A man in a wide-brimmed leather hat whispered to the auctioneer before he motioned for the next property to step forward. "Next up. A *pair*. A very healthy pair." The auctioneer smirked. Another boy sidestepped onto the platform, attached to a woman beside him. Two drudgers armed with popcap bombers stood beside the pair. They were the auction officiators who kept things from getting out of hand.

"Twelve years old. Strong. Defiant. Claims *he* and this *woman* are married—official-like—in the eyes of the Great Above." The auctioneer raised his palms skyward. "The woman don't talk, so I won't press my luck with Judas. These two stay together. Do whatever you want with the boy. *After* the sale."

Myron knew little of Judas except that he was the guardian spirit of betrayers and traitors. A real marriage would involve the blessing of Judas so that the couple would stay true to one another.

"Let's get going." Rounder eyed the sun's location in the

sky—it was dipping toward the horizon. "Hurry." Rounder motioned for the twins and their mother to return to the landship. Myron detected panic in Rounder's voice.

The whisper of the crowd turned into chatter as they inched toward the couple. Myron couldn't take his eyes off the auction, noting that even in his grandfather's stories of married people and families and the like, twelve was much younger than he'd expected a husband to be.

"This here woman, seventeen, maybe eighteen. *Very* healthy. A prize for sure."

The crowd erupted into a frenzy, calling out items to bid before the auction even started. A drudger shoved the woman to the front of the platform, the boy chained to her dragging along with her.

"Work the pedals. I'll get the sail ready." Rounder tightened the rope on the supplies.

The scene on the platform stole Myron's breath. He reached for the telescope in Rounder's belt.

"What are you—" Rounder's hand clamped down on the empty spot on his belt where the telescope had been.

The blur of the heads in the crowd whipped by in the lens as Myron centered the telescope on the auction platform. He closed his left eye and honed in on a vision that reminded him of his first day in Jonesbridge, after the stretcher, the first time he saw her—the brave girl who fought the guards with confidence, as if she had a chance of beating them. He would never forget her face, though, with time, his memories had blurred her features the way the telescope had.

"Sindra."

CHAPTER NINE

The telescope dropped from Myron's hand. The jumble of bidders pushed toward the merchandise—the love of Myron's life and the twelve-year-old kid claiming to be her husband. Myron leaped from the landship, navigating the crush of people who were offering as much as ten gallons of water, metal, wheels, vehicles, boilers, and all manner of valuables.

"Sindra!" Myron cupped his hands around his mouth and yelled, "Sindra!" She didn't hear him over the noise.

"Myron." Rounder pointed toward the southwest. "We don't have much time," he yelled.

"Sindra!" This time Myron sucked in a deep breath and bellowed her name. She glanced up from her fixed gaze on the ground.

"Myron?" Her eyes came to life.

The auctioneer paused his call. "Well, listen to that. She talks after all. But that won't lower the asking price." The auctioneer held his hand above his eyes as a visor, squinting in Myron's direction to see who'd interrupted the auction.

The crowd turned to look at Myron. He ran to the landship, untied the knot, and took inventory of everything he saw. "I've got water," he yelled. "Eleven gallons. Blankets. Food. Books. Whatever it'll take."

Rounder jogged up behind Myron and clapped his hand over his mouth.

"No he doesn't. That's not his stash. No bid." Rounder fought to keep his hand over Myron's mouth and keep him under control. "What the Chasm are you doing?" he whispered in Myron's ear. "We'll find you a girl if that's what you want. This one's too expensive."

Gah-té and Mah-ré watched Myron struggling. They looked at each other and came up behind Rounder. Gah-té reached into a bag and crumpled a handful of dried leaves between her fingers. She spat into her hands, mixing her saliva and the leaves into a green mud, while Mah-ré tapped Rounder on the shoulder. When Rounder turned toward Mah-ré, Gah-té came up from behind and cupped her hand filled with the mud over Rounder's nose and mouth, holding it there until he released Myron and fell to the ground with his eyes closed.

Myron eyed Rounder in a ball at his feet.

"Going once," the auctioneer bellowed. "Going twice."

"Ten shotgun shells," Myron yelled. The crowd gasped.

The auctioneer nodded. "We have a big spender."

"Eleven," a voice said from the other side of the mob.

Myron stood on his tiptoes for a look at who had outbid him and then dropped to his knees behind the landship.

Three Jonesbridge ghosts sat in a steam wagon with their eyes on Sindra.

"This just got interesting." The auctioneer stroked his patchy beard and studied the new arrivals. "Got some rich Alliance interlopers what want a go at this lovely." He strode over to Sindra and raised her arm, and the boy's raised with it. "Yes sir, this is what you want? She's yours if you're offering a shotgun to go with those shells."

"One shotgun," the ghost yelled.

Myron reached for Rounder's shotgun, and keeping his head down so the orange shirts couldn't see his face, he held it over his head. "I've got one too."

"Come to think of it, you don't see a woman like this here carpie every day. Maybe I'll keep her for myself."

"She's my wife," the boy beside Sindra yelled.

With the butt of his weapon, the drudger struck the boy from behind, just above the knee, causing his leg to buckle. "Enough. This carpie's your foggin' wife. You told us already."

Gah-té spat into her hands, mixing another batch of green mud. Her mother, who'd occupied herself during the stop by crafting a jade ringlet, fell back, eyes closed as Gah-té covered her mouth and nose with the mud as she'd done to Rounder.

Seeing her mother unconscious, Mah-ré stood as high as she could get on the landship. "*Dosh kant*!" she yelled.

All eyes in the crowd turned toward Myron and the twins. The auctioneer turned in the direction of the orange shirts. "Unless you got two Gapi girls to add to your bid, sale goes to the young man in the desert glider."

Gah-té and Mah-ré held hands and walked toward the auctioneer, glancing back at Myron.

The head ghost cocked his shotgun. "That girl up there has an Industry brand. She's ours."

"You should've held onto her, then."

"Who's going to stop us from taking her?"

"Her new owner, I reckon." The auctioneer pointed to Myron. "And—*Megan.*" He chuckled as he said her name.

Myron slipped on Rounder's work gloves to hide the Industry brands on his hands as the auction drudgers began the process of offloading everything Myron had paid for Sindra: eleven gallons of water, almost every drop Rounder had, one shotgun, all the shells Rounder had acquired at the depot, two blankets, five candles, a rope, a tarp, four shanks, a spare wheel, ten chunks of copper ore, a bag of prairie bread, six iron spikes, a figurine of a dancing woman carved from smooth black wood, and an amethyst gemstone. After the auctioneer loaded the goods onto the seller's wagon, he clamped Mah-ré and Gah-té in irons and handed them over to a man with a stub for an arm and a deep scar that ran the length of his face from the top of one side to the bottom of the opposite side, making a ridge through his nose.

Myron ran up to Sindra, hugging her. The chains between her and the boy rattled. The boy yanked Sindra back and gave Myron a shove.

"Don't touch my wife."

"She's not your wife." Myron pushed the kid back so hard that he fell, taking Sindra with him.

"Yes, she is."

"Sindra? Is this true?"

"Myron. I can't believe you're here. I never thought I'd see—"

"Sindra, is it true? Are you married to this kid?"

Sindra's gaze fell as she nodded.

"What? How—"A fist pummeled Myron from behind.

Rounder, still groggy, punched Myron across the face. He pushed him to the ground, striking him over and over.

"Myron." Sindra yanked the binding chains, pulling Nico with her. Rounder fell back. Myron stumbled to his feet and backed away, wiping the blood from his mouth.

"What did I tell you about thieves? What?" Rounder grabbed Myron by the throat. From behind, Sindra kicked Rounder between the legs, doubling him over. He moaned and fell to his knees. "You gave them everything. You stole it and gave it to them."

Myron took Sindra's hand. "I know her. She…we are—" Myron would have said they were in love, finally united and that they might take official vows in the eyes of the Great Above, but looked at the twelve-year-old kid chained to her in a dozen places and realized that his dreams had flushed again. "She's Industry." He showed Rounder the back of Sindra's hands. "Like you and me."

Rounder stood up, and grabbed Sindra's hands. He glanced at them, dropped them, and hung his head, returning to his empty landship where the twins' mother had awakened. She screamed her daughters' names, wailing, raising her hands, smacking Rounder in the back of the head over and over. Rounder took the blows, pointing to Myron and Sindra.

"I'm sorry." Blood sprayed from Myron's lips as he spoke.

Rounder sat in the landship, head bowed, rubbing his face, mumbling a half-Gapi rant, but Myron caught enough of what Rounder said to understand their predicament. Without supplies, they were stuck in Megan's Point.

CHAPTER TEN

"This is easy. One of them's already in chains." The Jonesbridge ghost said as two others stepped up to Rounder's landship. They inspected Sindra's hand, then Myron's. "*Two* runoff slogs. Some major shirking going on here."

"Three." The other ghost lifted Rounder's hand.

"Three? Whore's hairpin. The shirker motherlode. And some kid as a bonus." He grabbed Sindra's and Nico's chains and began leading them away. The other one pushed Myron behind her.

Rounder lifted his head with a smile. "Thief!" He stood and pointed to the three orange shirts. The crowd grew silent, except for the slowing creak of the windmills, and the lights flickering off and on as the power supply diminished.

The head ghost raised his shotgun to two approaching drudgers, not seeing the four behind him. "She ain't your property." The drudger pushed Sindra and Myron back in the direction of the landship.

"Yes she is. They all are." He tapped the back of his hand. "They bear the mark of Industry."

"That don't mean a bit of shat here." Four more drudgers arrived. "Megan's is the only law here."

"Not for long," the head ghost quipped.

Now outnumbering the ghosts ten to one, the drudgers escorted the ghosts to a wooden door behind the auction platform.

In the fracas, the twins' mother had gone in search of her daughters. Myron heard her screaming their names, and each time he heard them, her cries stung Myron with the reality of what he'd done.

"I'm so glad to see you." Sindra did not make eye contact with Myron.

"Who is this kid?" Myron gave Sindra's young husband a push on the shoulder.

"His name is Nico. And it's not what you think."

With the striations of purple and pink from the setting sun, in the chill of the desert at night, the breeze came to a complete stop. The blades of the largest of the windmills groaned to a halt. The lights of the town blinked off, leaving violet silhouettes of a growing crowd in the town center.

"Power!" a deep voice yelled from a high window on the west side of the stage.

Shadowy figures shuffled through the crowd to a steam locomotive on pylons five feet off the ground, something Myron had taken for an ornament. They stoked the smoldering coals in the firebox, shoveling in fresh fuel while another man filled the locomotive boiler with slick. The wheels on the locomotive turned, and, instead of pulling the weight of a train down the tracks, the churning wheels of the suspended locomotive powered the electrical generator turbines.

A puff of smoke came out of the locomotive chimney. The wheels sped up as two men shoveled coal into the firebox. A whoosh of steam released as the familiar chug of a locomotive pushed a roiling cloud of smoke out the chimney, which settled on the stage in the still air and flowed into the crowd as though a fog had rolled in.

Lights popped on one by one around the town center, all aimed at the bandstand. A floodlight, tinted green, switched on over the bandstand, growing brighter until it exploded into a shower of glass and sparks. One of the men feeding the locomotive its coal dropped his shovel and ran into the building behind the stage. He returned minutes later, positioned a three-story ladder against the central support of the tent over the stage in the town center, and replaced the bulb.

The Gapi merchants closed up their market stalls, shuttering the windows and locking the doors. They dispersed while everyone else headed toward the town center. Vendors and their apprentices joined stable hands and laborers, families, wanderers, and drudgers cramming into the plaza, vying for a spot near the platform, until they spilled over into darkened alleyways. Children sat on parents' shoulders. Overflow perched atop their stalls for a better view as the sun dipped below the horizon.

A hoarse whisper from the crowd began chanting Megan's name. "May-gun. May-gun." Two voices, then three, joined in, until the throng in the center of town chanted in unison, "May-gun, May-gun, May-gun." The smell of rot onion and rat wine filled the air.

"Supplies or not, we gotta get out of here. Megan's coming." Rounder pulled at the landship, trying to dislodge it from the people leaning on it for a better view of the bandstand.

The chant grew louder until it erupted into a deafening roar when a column of flames shot up from a pipe on the back of the bandstand.

"Oh, no." Rounder rubbed his face. "What did I say? One foggin' doughnut. In and out? I *know* that's what I said. Now we got nothing. No supplies. No water. No shotgun. And—" The thunder of the crowd smothered Rounder's words.

The steam, the lights, the crowd, spiraled together around Sindra's face, whose jaw fell when she saw the spectacle.

A spotlight hit the wall of steam over the stage. Dressed in a blue robe, Megan swept in on a rope swing, her long black hair wrapped around her neck. Sitting, legs crossed, she wore red shoes that drew the eye to her feet and then to the bare flesh of her legs. She arched her back and pulled up, sending the swing out over the crowd. Every eye followed her back and forth, higher and higher, as she absorbed the adulation. When the swing slowed, she hopped out and raised her hands.

"How's business?" Megan preened.

The responses ranged from cheers to shouts that jumbled together in a collective affirmation that commerce was alive and well in Megan's Point.

A procession marched onto the stage carrying three bound men, the orange shirts from Jonesbridge that Myron had encountered after the auction. They dropped the ghosts at Megan's feet. The frenzied crowd calmed. The town center grew quiet, except for the chug of the locomotive.

Megan kicked one of the ghosts in the ribs. "These three cockrels were caught trying to steal—in *my* town."

The rabble cheered.

"In *my* foggin' town." Megan tossed her hair over her shoulder. "Then, they questioned my authority. And do you know what these taint-licking shaggers told my drudgers?" She strolled across the stage, her robe gaping open to reveal a colorful scarf tight around her waist. "That this is my town—*for now.*" She whipped her arm into the air. "What should we do to them?" She cupped her hand around her ear and leaned toward the crowd.

Voices erupted with ideas, shouting over one another which punishment they wanted to see. Megan held up her hand and nodded, gesturing to her drudgers. The drudgers attached cables to the bound feet of the three orange shirts. Another drudger turned a crank, and the three ghosts, bound and gagged, rose upside down over the stage.

"The people have spoken. The Piñata it is."

A chorus of cheers mixed with hisses and boos.

Myron glanced at Sindra. He could see in her eyes, in her tears and her smile, satisfaction at seeing justice done to some Jonesbridge ghosts, like those who'd caused her pain.

Megan held out her hand. One of her drudgers jogged to a storage chest and returned with a weapon composed of a long wooden handle connected by a chain to a spiked iron ball. She pulled the sash from her robe, waving it toward the crowd with one hand while she spun the spiked ball over her head with the other. "Who wants first crack at the piñatas?"

The three orange shirts, faces turning red from hanging

upside down, squirmed and swung, trying to shake their bindings loose. Gagged with burlap, their muffled screams resembled grinding pistons low on oil. Megan eyed the sea of faces all pleading for a chance to join her on the stage.

She shielded her eyes from the bright spotlight and peered to the edges of the crowd. "Are you out there, Jasper? I heard you were here. You can't hide from me."

Rounder mumbled a string of expletives, hiding his face.

"I know my best drudger is out there somewhere."

"I don't work for you anymore," Rounder shouted.

"There you are." Megan snapped in Rounder's direction.

Within moments, a crew of drudgers pushed Rounder up to the bandstand to the cheers and calls of the restless throng. Megan ran her fingers across Rounder's chest while another drudger cinched a blindfold around Rounder's eyes. "I've missed you, Jasper." She rubbed her thigh up Rounder's leg.

"It's Rounder."

"*Rounder?*" Megan emitted a long, open-mouthed laugh aimed at her audience. "How cute." She placed the handle of the flail into Rounder's hand. Two drudgers spun him slowly while the crowd in the background chanted, "Piñata! Piñata!"

"I'm done killing for you, Megan." Rounder dropped the flail.

"You've said that before—yet here you are."

Rounder pulled the blindfold off his eyes. "This time, I'm done." Three drudgers blocked his path as he walked toward the steps of the bandstand.

"I heard a nasty rumor." Megan pointed to the ground. Two drudgers hit Rounder in the back of the knee, causing his knees to buckle, kneeling him before Megan. "That's better. On your knees." She motioned to the audience for applause. "I know it can't be true—that you're working for Te Yah at Mesa Gap?"

Rounder stared at the floor. "I've never even set foot in that place."

"You disappoint me, Jasper. Now, play piñata!" She stepped on his back and pushed his face all the way to the floor. "Yes?"

"Will you let me go?"

"If that's what you want. But I know what you *really* want." She straddled him, lowering herself onto him, whispering into his ear.

She lifted off of Rounder and the drudgers helped him to his feet, handing him the flail. Megan blindfolded him again, and the drums played a slow beat in rhythm with Rounder's spin.

"Don't do it, Rounder!" Myron shouted. "Don't kill them."

"Myron, what are you doing?" Sindra whispered.

"Who said that?" Megan whipped up her hand, and the drums halted midbeat.

"Thieves die in my town. Maybe you should join them."

"Let them go." Myron waited for inspiration, for anything to say that wouldn't dribble from his mouth like ooze from a leaky grease gun. "Back—back to Jonesbridge—where they'll tell everyone of your power."

Megan nodded, striding across the bandstand. "What a delicious idea." She sent her drudgers to retrieve Myron. "But one survivor is all it takes to tell the tale."

"One might not make it back to Jonesbridge by himself." The drudgers shoved Myron onto the bandstand. Rounder shook his head, overt enough for Myron to understand he'd made a big mistake in opening his mouth.

"Look at *you.*" Megan slinked up to Myron. "Tall. Strong. You just might be my next…special drudger—now that Jasper has ruined his chance."

"I d—" Megan cut Myron off midsentence with a kiss. She pressed her breasts against his chest. Her lips moved with his. Her tongue entered his mouth. His legs tingled all the way to his groin as he swayed into Megan, forgetting for the moment where he was and what had happened.

Then Megan pulled away without warning and spun to the crowd. "I'll make you a deal. What's your name?"

"My—my name?"

"Your name?"

"Myron."

"Okay, *Myron.* I'll make you a deal." She placed the flail in his hand. "I will release *two* of these worthless tate sniffers—to warn any others that might follow. My good nature knows no bounds." The crowd cheered. "If you play piñata with…" She strolled down the line of her captives hanging by their feet over the stage. "This one." She slapped the belly of the orange shirt on the far left. His eyes grew wide. He shook his head. Myron could hear him pleading through the gag.

"Why kill any of them?"

"Why?" She turned to the crowd. "*Why kill thieves?*, he asks." She gestured with both hands for the crowd to respond. "That's right." Megan pressed up against Myron, bringing her lips a breath away from his, leaving panging Myron with guilt for hoping she would kiss him again, tempted to initiate it himself. Megan instead poked him in the nose. "Because we don't like them." She strolled back to watch the spectacle at a safe distance from blood splatter. "One for two. Now get going."

Seeing the orange uniforms of the Civility Administration—ghosts, cockrels, whatever name they took—in their current state, vulnerable and squirming, reminded Myron that they'd killed his mother, enslaved him, treated Sindra like carnal property, and done everything in their power to destroy any dreams that germinated. Myron gripped the flail and swung it around over his head.

"Don't do it, Myron!" Sindra yelled. "Myron!"

"Sindra." Myron lowered the flail.

"Oh, this just gets keeps getting better." Megan rolled her eyes. "My, my, the choice just got harder, *Myron.*"

In the corner of his eye, Myron caught Rounder mouthing something. Still in a kneeling position, Rounder held his hand to his mouth as if eating and mouthed the word enough times for Myron to understand—doughnut.

"In order to save the carpie you just bought in my auction…" Megan winked at the crowd. "Something tells me they already know each other." A few in the front row laughed nervously. "You will piñata all three thieves. Once you have done that, Rounder won't have to piñata the girl."

"Run, Sindra. Run."

Rounder mouthed *doughnut* again just to make sure Myron understood, and jumped to his feet in the chaos of drudgers who ran for Sindra. Chained together, Sindra and Nico made a coordinated dash into the dark market as though they had run in chains together before.

"Someone is going to play piñata." Megan pointed at two more drudgers who gave chase into the market.

Rounder ran for the wall to the left of the bandstand and slipped through a crack. Myron followed. As he reached the spot where Rounder had disappeared into the rubble of the Old Age building behind them, a blast sounded from above. Pain shot down Myron's back as the shrapnel from a drudger popcap grazed him in the back. Most of the debris hit the wall, but a large shard of glass wedged into Myron's shoulder blade.

A popcap exploded again and three people near the stage dropped, moaning, blood seeping from jagged wounds where the shrapnel tore holes in their bodies. "Doughnuts," Myron whispered. He squeezed through a crack in the Old Age building behind the bandstand, the glass in his back edging farther into his muscle, as he tried to recall where Rounder's aunt sold doughnuts. The market resembled a maze with more twists and turns than the Jonesbridge factory drainage canals.

With the bulbs in the market darkened, slits of moonlight ripped through seams in the fabric overhead. Myron trailed the fleeing shadow ahead of him, hoping it was Rounder. Noises from the town center echoed with shouts and cursing, pledges to dice into a thousand pieces everyone involved in the disruptions.

When he'd grown confident he could hide in the shadows, every light in the market illuminated at once, making it resemble daytime in the middle of the night. Myron froze. Ahead, Rounder darted around a corner.

Alone in the alley, Myron scanned the closed stalls in search of a place to hide.

"Psst," a voice whispered.

Myron turned to see an elderly Gapi man gesturing from

a small opening between the crumbling walls of two Old Age buildings. The man grabbed Myron's arm and tugged him into a recess through a fabric curtain that separated a clothing merchant and a pipe vendor.

Muffled footsteps and voices sounded from the alleyway. The man panicked, motioning for Myron to get down. He dug out an iron rod with a hexagonal tip on one end and fitted it into a receptacle jutting from the Old Age wall. He bent the rod where it hinged in the center and cranked. A chain ticked from inside the wall, while gears churned beneath. The giant loom where the weaver fashioned cloth rose to reveal a rusted iron disc emblazoned with the words SEWER ACCESS.

"*Baj paqua*," the man whispered. He pointed to the manhole cover and used the same iron rod to pry the lid open. A waft of smoke rose from under the lid. "*Baj*." He cocked his head toward the opening.

Myron glared down the hole. Once inside, he grasped the ladder and climbed down. The lid closed the circle of light above him. He heard the sound of the gears and chain lowering the loom that concealed the manhole. Myron prepared for darkness and uncertainty as he reached the bottom. Instead, he saw candlelight flickering and people gathered at an intersection of three tunnels.

In one tunnel, Myron found a handful of Gapi men huddled around a game of chance where they rolled a small wooden ball around a wheel and placed bets to see where the ball would stop. It looked more complicated than nub, the game slogs played for rations in the swill pen, which required no special equipment. This game used a wheel with symbols on the edge, holding the players breathless as the ball popped and rolled until it slid into a recess in the wheel, when a mishmash of cheering and cursing erupted, just short of a fight, as the winners collected their takes.

"How did I not know about this place?"

Myron jumped when he heard Rounder's voice. He turned to see Rounder following his aunt down the main tunnel.

"You were a drudger," his Aunt Ktala said. She placed a smoldering pipe between her lips and puffed, holding the smoke in her lungs for a moment before releasing it with a breath that smelled of burning rubber. "One way in, two ways out, and Megan doesn't know about it." Ktala clapped once. "Maybe it's not her town after all."

"Rounder." Myron ran up beside them and spotted Sindra. Their eyes met, Sindra looking over Nico's shoulder. Sindra ran for Myron, pushing Nico backward causing them both to stumble.

"Got to get rid of these crazy chains." Rounder slapped at the chains that tethered Sindra to her mysterious young husband in fourteen places. "All this clanking metal makes too much noise." He pointed to the shackle cuffs around Myron's ankles where four lengths of the cut chain dangled.

"Come on." Aunt Ktala nodded for them to follow her down the tunnel to a collection of people huddled around candles mending ripped clothing.

Ktala spoke to another old woman, who left and then returned with a ring of keys containing every shape, size, and type of key Myron could imagine. Some rusted, some shiny, some fashioned from Old Age alloys, she tried one after another on Myron's shackle cuff, working the keys in and out, jiggling, until the lock clicked and the cuff fell away.

"This one." She tossed Myron's shackle onto a pile of scrap metals. "Came from Jonesbridge. I know those well." When she spotted the glass in Myron's back, she placed a rag around the wound and slipped the glass from his flesh, pointing to Ktala to hold the cloth to stop the bleeding.

She lifted the chains between Sindra and Nico. "These are—strange. Haven't seen this type of mechanism before." She studied her keys, eyeing the shapes and examining the locks "Who put this on you?"

"Dromon coupled us up like this. In Orkin's Landing."

"Orkin's Landing?" Aunt Ktala took a sudden interest. "The ocean conclave?"

"Ocean everywhere."

"You saw the ocean?" Myron held the cloth on his back and sat beside Sindra while the locksmith worked her picks on Sindra's chain. "It's real?"

"Yeah, it's real. Water spilling over the horizon."

"Why did they chain you like this?" Rounder sat beside them working out how the crisscrossed chains that bound them together worked.

"It's a unity binding," Sindra said, never looking Myron in the eyes.

"What they do to married couples that won't consummate their union." Nico spat out the explanation with frustration.

"It's his fault we wound up like this. All he had to do was lie." Sindra squeezed Myron's hand.

"*My* fault? Carlisle couldn't even break us out of this. Wouldn't've mattered if I lied or not." Nico looked to the roof of the tunnel as if to stare through the arch of Old Age bricks above him. "Besides, you can't lie to the Great Above. He's the only one that can get us out of this thing."

"Me and Sindra had plans on joining," Myron said.

"Too late for that. We're joined in the eyes of Judas. That's forever," Nico said.

"I can't figure this lock." The woman clicked her tongue. "Strange. Forged stainless alloy. Good luck cutting it off, either. You kids might be stuck together for a good while."

Sindra groaned.

"The only way to get out of the binding is to…well, you know…make our marriage official with sexing."

"Right. And how's that going to get these chains off?"

"I don't know. That's what Dromon said."

"Dromon? You're too smart of a kid—"

"Why did you marry this kid?" Myron gave Nico a shove on the shoulder.

"You think I had a *choice?*"

"You had a choice." Nico nodded.

"Did you?" Myron pulled Sindra's face toward his so that their eyes met.

Sindra closed her eyes. "They stole my baby, Myron."

CHAPTER ELEVEN

Sindra awoke to the sight of Nico's face, his mouth gaping, his tongue like a slab of salted pork strap. Her own head rested on Myron's shoulder. His arms embraced her through the unity chains. She could no longer distinguish her own odor from Nico's or which one of them piqued the nose more, but Myron's smell brought her back to Jonesbridge, to a time when they dreamed together, planned their escape, and saw the world for the first time with promise instead of hopelessness.

Sindra shoved Nico, the same way she'd woken him up for the past five days, though sleep in the unity binding only came in fits of waking dreams. She moved Myron's arms to keep them from getting pinched by the chains. A fourth face, sucking the breath from the crowded jumble of people, the locksmith, studied the locking mechanism on Sindra's neck. From the looks of her eyes, red and watery, Sindra imagined that the old lady hadn't yet fallen asleep for the night.

"I don't think I can take this much longer." Sindra studied the folds in the old woman's face and wondered what it must be like to live so long at a time when Sindra feared she and Nico would spend the rest of their short lives breathing the same stale air.

Along the areas where the cuffs rubbed against her skin, red swollen patches filled with pus reminded her of the time she watched over Myron in the bunker as he slept with fever and nightmares and a bullet in his leg. Lalana's words haunted her then. "Specs too small to see can kill a man as sure as any piss whistle," she'd claimed. Lalana's warning resurfaced as Sindra noticed the same raw skin on Nico.

Ktala stood over them, next to Rounder. "I don't know anyone in the market that can take *that* off."

Myron's eyes opened. "There has to be a way."

"There is. Only one person I can think that has a chance at taking that thing off." Rounder pointed upward. "Ren."

"Ren?" Ktala squinted as if to study a reel of faces in her mind.

"Megan's concubine—mastermind behind all of her torture contraptions." Rounder bowed his head. "She's an expert contraptionist—with metals, gears, even electricity."

"Let's go. Where do we find her?" Myron untangled his arms from the chains.

"Whoa—you three cost me everything, the whole barrel of bolts, all I've collected the past few months. You spent my life savings buying these two chained-together rack warts, and now I got nothing. Nothing."

"I'm sorry, Rounder." Myron took Sindra's hands. Nico's followed. "Lalana took a bullet for me—so that I could find

Sindra. Her life, Sindra's life, everyone is worth more than a wagon full of junk."

"Junk? You're going to learn the hard way out here that wagons full of junk are the only way you survive in the Nethers."

Ktala placed her hands on Rounder's shoulders and turned him toward her. "I've known you since you were a baby, Jasper."

"Rounder. It's Rounder."

"Fine. Rounder it is. Makes no difference what I call you." She pointed a finger to his chest. "It's what's in here that matters. And you can help these poor kids."

"You were there last night. You saw Megan. That piñata bit might be the most humane thing I've seen her do in a while." He belted out a nervous laugh, waving toward the village above them. "She's a merchant through and through. A trader. And she don't take the short end of any deal. Whether or not Ren can even get them apart, Megan's gonna want something in return. Something big. And I ain't got nothing left to give her."

"I'd give her one of my body motors if she could get us apart." Sindra wasn't certain which of the essential body motors a person had two of or could live without, but rich people paid big money to eat such things as a delicacy. "Heart, liver, lungs, kidney—cut it out and take it, just get me the Chasm out of this thing."

"You need all those motors, dear," Ktala said. "Well—'cept lung and kidney. Got more than one of those."

"Besides, no one's paying to eat a slog motor. And she'd kill you getting it out."

"Okay, then what?" Sindra looked to Myron, hoping for an idea to pop out of his mouth.

"Megan likes you, Rounder. You were her drudger."

"So?"

"So...maybe you could offer to work for her ag—"

"No. No. No."

"Please take us to Ren." The whites of Nico's half-open eyes were the color of blood.

"Megan's drudgers are already looking for us after last night. And she sleeps during the day. And I ain't about to wake her."

"Please, Rounder. We're salvagers. We can help you replace what I spent to get Sindra." Myron helped Sindra and Nico to their feet. "We can go without you. We don't have to have your help."

Ktala spoke up before Rounder could respond. "Yes, you do. No one knows where Megan sleeps. No one else can get through her drudgers. And—without Rounder, she might just kill you for the fun of it."

Though Sindra had known Rounder for only a few hours, most of which she'd spent asleep, she was grateful that he had at least befriended Myron and that he'd had a wagon full of junk for Myron to spend on her. But those two girls, the twins—they were the ones who'd sacrificed for her, who'd given up their freedom, going willingly into slavery so that Myron could win the auction. If she and Nico were going to die anyway, how guilty she would feel in her last moments, making all of Myron's efforts pointless. "We have to try, Rounder. I'll go out there and raise the Chasm until I see her if I have to."

Rounder rubbed his face and cursed in Gapi under his

breath, to the disapproval of his Aunt Ktala. "I will take you to Ren. I won't talk to Megan. I won't work for Megan. I won't kill for Megan. Is that clear?"

"Okay." Myron nodded. "Thanks, Rounder."

"*Okay?* That's what you said when I told you we were coming down here for one doughnut. In and out, I said. I want more than *okay.*"

"We'll make our own deals. We promise," Sindra said.

Rounder cut a circle through the air with his index finger. The old woman locksmith and Ktala walked over to an alcove and pulled a rectangular box from the wall. The size of a shoe, the box had an earpiece on one end and, on the other, a cable that ran into a small hole in the wall. "*Sube,*" Ktala said into the receiver.

Rounder nodded in the direction of the ladder. Myron fell in behind him, and Sindra and Nico performed their travel ritual, which required Sindra to put aside her contempt for her familiarity of Nico and cooperate in lockstep, twins in an exposed womb made of chains, and now, they faced the ladder again, this time up instead of down.

Once they all came out on top, the loom over the manhole lowered, and Rounder bartered with the weaver for Gapi clothes. He had nothing to offer except promises of future items, which the weaver took for granted. With the sun rising, the markets of Megan's Point opened their stalls and set out merchandise, while the midnight rabble shuffled off to find a place to sleep. Rounder slipped on a duster. He burrowed his head into the hood, shadowing his face. Beside the stall, the weaver removed bolts of cloth from his rickshaw and motioned for Sindra, Nico, and Myron to load up. Rounder draped them in cloth in such a way that their limbs resembled bolts of cloth.

"Keep quiet in there." Rounder tapped Sindra on the back. "And try not to move."

The past few days, Sindra had acclimated to twisting and turning her body in unnatural ways to accommodate Nico's coordinated movements. At times she thought her ribs would punch through her stomach or her wrists would snap off from being bent the wrong way too far. Her neck ached of cricks on both sides that screamed when she turned her head. Her feet had grown numb, and, where the cuffs hadn't rubbed her skin into sores, calluses had formed. Not moving, as Rounder ordered, would have been a welcome change for her if the rickshaw bed had been larger or if they hadn't been arranged in such a way as not to have her head between her legs, the chains twisted, pinching her skin, and Nico's hand on her mouth.

"How long is this going to take?" Sindra whispered.

"I don't know. Be quiet."

Sindra could hear Rounder's labored breathing as he navigated the rickshaw through the maze of the Megan's Point market. He stopped, restarted, and stopped again. Sindra had only a minced view of their surroundings through the fabric.

"Listen up." Rounder poked his head under the cloth. "Myron, you first. There is a secret passageway to avoid Megan's guards. It's very narrow—"

"Oh," Sindra moaned.

"Do you want that thing off or not?" Rounder helped Myron out and pointed him to a crawlspace at the bottom of an Old Age wall. "This is tricky."

The sun stung Sindra's eyes when Rounder pulled back the cloth. She and Nico stepped out to a narrow alley not much wider than the rickshaw. They worked down to their knees, timing each movement until they lay flat on the ground, Nico on top of Sindra. Myron pushed them through the hole in the wall while Rounder pulled from the other side.

They squeezed through broken walls, climbed over debris, and snaked through holes, leading upward, until they hit a dead end at a wooden wall.

"Ren," Rounder whispered through a slit in the wall. "Ren? You there?" He waited with his ear up to the wall.

"Jasper?"

"We need your help."

"You can't be here."

"Please."

"What is it?" Ren opened a small square in the wall just big enough for her to see Rounder.

"This." Rounder shoved Sindra and Nico forward so that Ren could see the unity binding.

"Oh, wow. Where did you find that?"

"Forget that. How do we get them out of it?" Rounder held a finger to his lips. "And *please*—without waking Megan."

Ren, Megan's highest-ranking enforcer and concubine, laughed. "It'll cost you."

"What do you want?"

"I want *that.*" Ren jammed her hand through the rectangular opening and jutted her finger toward the unity binding.

"It's yours."

"And Jasper, you know that nothing happens around

here without Megan's consent. Megan's price will be... steeper than mine."

"Here we go." Rounder turned to Myron. "I figured."

Sindra wondered what Ren would want with such a terrible device. "How long will this take?"

Ren spat at Myron. "Tell your slave to keep quiet, or I will change my mind."

Sindra had not allowed herself to think about the reality of her situation, that Myron now owned her in the eyes of Nethers law, bought and paid for.

A series of clicks sounded from the other side of the wall before a heavy door eased open. Ren, wearing only a sheet, walked back over to Megan, who slept naked on a pair of giant pillows in the middle of a room. Alcoves and crannies edged the narrow chamber that concealed the Old Age decay of the structure with throws and rugs covering the floor, tapestries hanging from the walls, scarves draped from sconces and waves of purple satin festooned from the ceiling. Electric bulbs splashed yellow light across the room, exploding the colors into blotches of bright and shadow.

Megan's eyes opened. She stood without regard to having a crowd stand before her while she strode across the room naked. She slipped on a black shawl. When she pulled it taut, cinching it around her waist, a pair of pointed red wings spread behind her back. "I knew you'd be slithering back to my bed sooner or later, Jasper."

"I—" Megan placed her finger on Rounder's lips before he could speak and walked right past him.

"Before we get started..." she pressed up against Myron. "I did let my adoring public play piñata, but I allowed one of those cockrels, as you suggested, crawl back to Jonesbridge with injuries that will tell his tale." She ran her fingers over Sindra's arm, up her neck, stopping to caress her face. She pulled Sindra's chin toward her. "Aren't you a plucky sight." A smile spread across her face as her hands found the chains of the unity binding, her fingers walking along the links like the Orkinites on rope bridges. "And this—is outrageous."

Ren grabbed an iron ring holding a single key. She held out her hand to swipe the fabric on the walls as she meandered through Megan's sleep chamber to a metal door with a small window made of thick glass. She twisted the key in the door's lock. The door swung open.

The wings on Megan's robe fluttered as she walked, swinging her hips. "Before Ren takes care of your problem, there's a little matter of payment."

"I already offered the binding as payment." Rounder took a deep breath.

Sindra's salvage instincts kicked in; she imagined how valuable the Old Age metal in the binding was and how the salvage factory in Jonesbridge would have congratulated her if she'd brought such a find to their attention.

"And I'm thrilled to see what Ren can do with it. Or, who she can do with it." Megan placed her arm across the open metal door. "Maybe I'll bind you and me in this thing together." Megan ran her fingernail down Myron's chest, leaving a scratch that threatened to bleed.

Megan's long fingernails sharpened to a point and reminded Sindra of an imp tongue. "But Ren is my property," Megan said. "She works on what I want her to work on."

"Of course." Rounder shut his eyes.

"Ren will free these two for…" Megan pointed her finger at Myron, then Rounder, and Sindra.

"You." Megan pointed to Nico. "You're a bit fragile, but you'll do. A nice clean slate to work with. If I can't train you to be a champion drudger, you can be my personal attendant."

"No." Sindra wedged in front of Nico. "He can't stay with you. He's a kid."

"Please, no." Nico's eyes welled with tears. "I have to go home."

"Are you volunteering to take his place?" Megan twirled a lock of Sindra's hair as she inspected her curves.

"Sindra, what are you doing?" Myron grabbed her arm and pulled her close, yanking Nico as well.

"He's an innocent kid, Myron. Think—what'll happen to him if he stays with her."

"Oh, I'm not that bad." Megan cocked her hip. "Once he gets a little older, believe me, he'll have the time of his life."

"Nope." Rounder shook his head and stepped in front of Nico. "Sindra's right, Myron."

"Oh, you're just jealous of this young blood." Megan slapped Rounder on the chest.

Myron doubted that Nico's virtue would last another day in the Nethers whether he stayed with Megan or not. Weighed against the price already paid for Myron to reunite with Sindra, what was the value of Nico's innocence? Lalana had given her life for Myron to find Sindra, the twins had sold themselves into slavery, Rounder had lost everything, all for Myron and Sindra to be together again, and now, protecting some kid who'd enjoyed the splendor of growing up near the sea threatened to derail Myron's plans even more. That kid had already stolen the love of Myron's life by marrying her in the eyes of the Great Above. There was no way back from that. According to the law of Megan's

Point, Myron owned both Nico and Sindra. He could veto Sindra's decision.

"So what'll it be? The kid?" Megan held out her left hand in front of Nico. "Or the carpie?" She opened her other hand in front of Sindra.

"Sindra isn't a carpie." Myron gritted his teeth.

"Tell yourself that if you like. I don't care." Megan ran her finger down Sindra's cheek.

"Take Nico," Myron said.

"No. Take me." Sindra closed her eyes.

"Oh, I will. You can bet on it." Megan winked. "Now, get them out of this delicious device."

"Myron, it's okay. We have to get out of this thing." Sindra's voice sounded weak. She strained to lift her head.

Megan patted Sindra's lips with her hand. "Don't speak, girl. I will let you know when you can speak." Megan stepped aside and extended a hand of welcome through the metal door.

"No. This is where I stop." Rounder backed up. "I'm never going in there again."

"Jasper, you wound me. After all the fun we've had together?"

Sindra and Nico passed through the doorway with Myron leading the way into a circular chamber with a high ceiling. The wall was black, the floor red. Hundreds of shards of broken mirrors on the ceiling twinkled as Ren lit the torches on the walls. What the torchlight revealed left Sindra with a lump in her throat.

Chains hung from the ceiling in different lengths, some with barbed hooks, some with cuffs, some crisscrossing to pulleys weighted with stones. Under the chains sat slabs equipped with restraints and stretching mechanisms, hooks and feathers, blades in the shapes of crescent moons and harnesses that looked as though they would contort the body in impossible ways. Splatters of blood stained the black walls, and while the red floor had absorbed most of the color, the brown outline of blood persisted in dried pools. When the door shut behind them, Sindra lost hope, and felt she would rather die with Nico in the binding than become Megan's gory pleasure toy.

Ren motioned for Nico and Sindra to follow her to a workbench surrounded on three sides by tool bins and welding equipment. She flipped a switch that turned on a set of lights, brightening the table. She placed the nearest locking mechanism on the table, causing Sindra and Nico to twist and bend to accommodate her positioning. She muttered under her breath, moving the cylinder on the lock back and forth. "This is a cipher lock. Each one is different. Better bring a cask of scog." She put on her jeweler's lenses and placed a stethoscope earpiece into her ears. She positioned the diaphragm onto the lock.

Sindra guessed that Ren had twisted, probed, picked, turned, and cursed at the mechanism for at least a half an hour before anyone heard a click. The cuff and chain tethering their necks fell away to dangle on Nico's chest. She made quicker work of the lock on the cuff around Nico's neck. When it unhinged, Ren set aside the first of fourteen chains and took a swig of scog.

Megan went back to her sleeping chamber to rest. Myron wandered the black room, studying the devices. After each lock, Ren downed more scog, slowing her progress. Unable to see the sun or sky in the black room, Sindra couldn't tell whether it took all day or all night, until the last chain gave way just when Megan returned, refreshed and ready for her nightly show on the city stage. Sindra rubbed her forearm and scratched the red, swollen bands of skin where the cuffs had worn sores into her flesh. Ren finished off the scog and passed out on the floor.

As soon as Ren completed the separation of Nico and Sindra, Myron embraced Sindra. They kissed, and Myron, recalling the way Megan had kissed him on the stage, opened his mouth in the same way, a real kiss that he and Sindra now shared.

"Oh no." Megan wrenched them apart and stepped between them. "She's my property now. Fair warning: next time you do that it'll be theft of services. And everyone knows what happens to thieves in Megan's Point."

CHAPTER TWELVE

Megan's preparation for her nightly performance mesmerized Myron. She sat before a mirror brushing colors and powders onto her eyes and cheeks, and fiddled with her hair, twisting it into a thick braid that she tied with a black ribbon. She paraded around her chamber naked, until she selected a tunic from a heap of clothing and slipped it on. From a scattering of shoes, she carefully plucked a pair that had knife blades for heels.

Nico's eyes were as wide open as his mouth as Megan sashayed around the room. Ren, too, attended Megan with her bleary gaze. Rounder faced Megan's direction, but his eyes were closed.

Sindra's hands were cuffed to a leash, attached to a pole in the center of the room. She was able to move about, but only a few feet from the pole.

"Don't look at him." Megan snapped her fingers at Sindra. "You look at *me*." Sindra lowered her head. She was relieved to be free from the binding, but she had no more energy for a fight.

"Please, ma'am, can I go home now?" Nico said. "I don't belong here."

"'Fraid not, kid." Megan pointed to Myron. "You're his, now."

"Myron, please."

"You can't make it out there on your own, Nico. You better stay with us for now." Myron gave him a pat on the back.

"I can get you as far as Mesa Gap," Rounder said.

"This little merry pack of men is too funny," Megan said to Ren. "They act like they're going to get to leave Megan's Point."

Ren managed a nervous laugh.

Bora Bora. It had to be with Sindra, and it had to be with her baby. He had to make it, and they had to come with him, not stay in Megan's Point or be raised in the dungeon of some fanatic on the coast, or exist as some toy for a maniacal warlord. Myron had more luck formulating a plan when he allowed the idea to find him. All day his mind had raced over how to get out of this mess, how to free Sindra, escape Megan, and rescue Sindra's baby. His conclusion: impossible, more impossible, unknown level of impossibility, but impossible nonetheless. His grandfather would have told him that impossible meant just that, qualifying it made no sense. And he would have reminded Myron that nothing was impossible, but Myron's despair and disappointment with life on the other side of the Great Gorge had addled his thinking.

When the idea materialized, a surge of energy struck. "Sindra's your property now, right?"

"We made a deal. No backing out now."

"Right. So if someone stole from Sindra, they'd be stealing from you, right?"

Megan's face reddened. "Yes."

"Well, that's what's happened. Someone stole her baby." If this worked, he could rescue the baby and get Nico home, and he and Sindra could make a run for Bora Bora.

"A *baby*?" Megan's lip curled. "This cute band of travelers just gets more interesting by the hour."

"They stole from Sindra—so they stole from you. Will you avenge your property?"

"Oh, you *are* an operator." Megan gathered her hair into a bundle that she slung over her shoulder. "You look like a yummy biscuit, but you're dangerous. So full of *ideas,* aren't you?" Wearing her shoes heeled with knife blades made her as tall as Myron. He felt his entire body tingle as she approached, hoping she would touch him and hating himself for it. "First of all, who are our alleged thieves?"

"Orkin," Sindra said.

Ren stood and backed into a corner away from Megan.

Rage built in Megan's eyes, as though someone had loaded her firebox with too much coal. "Orkin. *The* Orkin?" She removed one of her shoes, closed one eye, and hurled the shoe at the wall where it stuck in the wood by the heel, inches away from Ren's head. "I knew I should have killed him when I had the chance."

"Kill Orkin?" Nico shook his head. "He's the voice of the Great Above on earth."

"He's a taint-sniffing dog in bed with an imp from the Chasm, as sure as he worships the Great Above."

Nico winced as though calamity or lightning might strike at any moment. "He's our father." Nico's eyes welled with tears.

"And he bound you to a witch and got rid of you." Sindra pulled at the chain that tethered her to the pole.

"You're a witch?" Megan paused, revealing a moment of concern.

Sindra waited to answer, until all eyes landed on her. "Maybe."

Megan placed her hand on Nico's head. "Oh, I know. I, too, grew up in Orkin's Landing with the *father*. If they could only see me now." She twirled with her hand over her head. "But, technically, the theft took place before she was my property—and out of my domain."

"Can't you ever just do something…nice? Just once? Always, 'what's in it for me? What do I get out of it? Who do I get to watch scream and cry for mercy?'" Rounder said.

"I do, Jasper. You're still alive, aren't you?"

"Great. Thanks for that. Now, as long as you're being so generous, I go by Rounder now. Jasper is dead. I'm never killing for your sport again."

Hearing Rounder's voice booming, a drudger opened the door, and, without looking inside the room, said, "Everything okay in there?"

"I don't know. Is everything okay?" Megan said to Rounder as she yanked her shoe from the wall. The knives in her heels stabbed holes in the pillows on the floor as she stomped toward the door. Gray fluffs floated from the ruptured pillows and drifted through the lamplight.

"Well?" Myron asked.

"What would I want with a baby? And what's my property to you? Baby or no baby, she's mine until the buzzards peck out her eyes." Megan pointed to Sindra. "And so is her baby if I go after Orkin for it."

"Please."

Megan stopped short of the door. The chant from the throng gathered in the town square had begun. "May-gun, May-gun, May-gun." She whipped around and stared at Myron. "Orkin has been a dead man to me since I left that place. Now, he is a thief. And he deserves a thief's death." She glanced at her fingernails, returning to the cool character her fans would expect. "Preferably on my stage. But Orkin is powerful. If you can convince Te Yah, another selfish thief, to help with a battle against Orkin, I will get the baby back."

"And what about Sindra?"

Megan sighed. "You can buy her freedom if, by whatever means necessary, you retrieve what Te Yah stole from me."

"What is it?"

"It doesn't matter." Rounder patted Myron on the back. "It is a fool's mission. Mesa Gap is a fortress. An unknown. And Te Yah can see right into your soul."

"What is it, you ask? It is an energy source with enough power to light the night sky. Orkin wants it. Jonesbridge wants it. The League wants it. I had it. Te Yah took it."

"My guess is that Te Yah didn't steal that from you. He's not really that sort."

"Oh, *Rounder*, you're not calling *me* a thief, are you? Because that will land you on stage tonight with the crowd splattered in your blood."

"It's just that I been from the bowels to the armpit and

back of the Nethers, turning through Old Age garbage and ruins. Never seen anything working proper. And I never ran across anything that could light the night sky." Rounder took a breath. "And I ain't calling you a liar or thief. I wouldn't do that. I'm not stupid."

"Te Yah took it from me. I want it back." She cocked her ear toward the chanting crowd. "I can't keep them waiting." She motioned for the drudgers to escort Rounder, Myron, and Nico out of the building. "I have decided to let you go. On the outside chance that you try."

"What should I say to Te Yah to get him to help?" Myron asked.

"Chasm knows. He won't talk to me." Megan erupted in laughter. "Oh, and I've had that little back door passageway blocked up, so don't think about coming back that way, Rounder."

The drudgers tugged on Myron's arm and led them out to the town center, lit up for Megan's show. Rounder shielded his view of the stage with his hand as he walked toward the dark market with Myron and Nico trailing behind him, heads down.

"You know, there are times I think back to that poor scrub on the other end of that chain when I found you out on the flat." Rounder marched into the darkness of the market with his face buried in his hands. "That Gapi woman was right about you. She lost her girls. I lost everything. Your woman's up there in the last place she's gonna be." He turned around and grabbed Myron by the shoulders. "Chained up with that dead man. She was right. You cheated death. Now it's coming for vengeance—on all of us. We'll wish we was dead by the time this is done. I want you to disappear. Go the Chasm away from me. I don't care where you go. I don't give a squat what you do, just go away and take your bad muji away from me. Go." He took Nico's hand. Nico's arms and legs bore red bands from the cuffs, where the skin was torn and oozing. "I'm gonna take this kid to Ktala and let her fix these wounds."

Myron thought of Sindra's sacrifice for Nico's innocence and figured that spending too much time with Rounder would also dampen the light in the kid's eyes. "No. Nico's coming with me." Myron stepped between Rounder and Nico.

"Fine."

"I'm sorry, Rounder." Myron searched his memory for any bits of wisdom left from his grandfather.

"You're sorry? I shoulda let you die with your partner out there."

"Saul was *not* my partner. He was lower than a rock lizard."

Rounder cracked his knuckles. "I don't care who he was. Or if he was an okay guy. What I'm saying is you should've died with him. End of tale. Bones sandblasted by the Nethers."

"But I need help with Te Yah. I don't even know where Mesa Gap is."

"Oh, forget that. You can't get in there. You can't see Te Yah. You're done. You're the walking dead."

"What's in Mesa Gap? How do you get in?"

"I told you that I refused to take the intention ritual. Well, that's not true. I did take it, and Te Yah didn't find my intentions honorable. Okay? I don't know what's in there, or how to get in. Go if you want to. I have to rebuild my life savings thanks to you."

As Rounder left and the darkness of the market alley absorbed his silhouette, Myron paced from one closed vendor to the next, determined to scheme a way to make right at least some of this predicament.

Myron turned to Nico. "This man Orkin, what does he want with Sindra's baby?" They headed the opposite direction of Rounder to find someone who could tell them how to get to Mesa Gap.

"He thinks that a baby born to an unclean mother must be raised under strict spiritual guidance. Else, the baby will fall to the deeds of the mother."

"Sindra is not unclean."

Megan had the protection of scores of drudgers. They guarded her quarters and flanked her stage. They stalked the shadows above the market and peered through the broken windows of the Old Age ruins that lorded over Megan's Point. The only task Myron could imagine more daunting than rescuing Sindra, a theft against Megan, would be rescuing Sindra's baby from some fanatical preacherman named Orkin. Sindra, now Megan's possession, had made the twins' gesture of voluntary servitude all in vain. If Myron dared steal anything from anyone in Megan's Point, he would free the twins and return them to their mother. That was one thing he could do.

Myron and Nico found a hidden alcove to spend the night in. They awoke at first light to the patter of feet shuffling through the market, of doors and windows opening, and Gapi murmurings between merchants preparing their wares. Myron went from stall to stall seeking anyone he could communicate with, pleased that many vendors spoke both his language and Gapi. The first few he queried about Mah-ré and Gah-té didn't want to speak of them. The next few wouldn't. He finally learned that the slaver who had received them as payment for Sindra and Nico had sold them the next day to the refuser, whose job it was to rid the market of waste and garbage at the end of the day.

"That's an awful vocation, the 'refuser,'" Nico said.

With the help of a few vendors, Myron located the refuser shed on the edge of the market and watched it from behind the mule stable on the other side of the alley. The refuser had a bald head with one bushy eyebrow and a hairless scar where the other should have been. His cheek bulged with billet thistle that compelled him to spit a milky green blob every few minutes, a mess that qualified as waste, adding to what needed cleaning.

When Mah-ré came out of the shed with a broom, Myron noticed the twins' mother working alongside them. Myron resolved to get all three of them to Mesa Gap. Nico, too.

He inspected the drudger catwalks that crisscrossed above the market. Two drudgers surveyed the activity going on below. With so many people moving about in the alleys, Myron decided to wait until Megan's show, when the market darkened and the noise emanated from the town center, when the streets emptied and the refuser crew went to work.

As the evening hours turned to twilight, the refuser slammed open the shed door, cursing. He slapped the twins' mother when she didn't respond fast enough to his demands, then shoved the twins out and tethered each of their wrists to a pole with a lamp on the end that he carried while they did the cleaning. Myron did not see the exact location of the refuser's key, but he would have plenty of time to search the shed with them all out cleaning.

"Nico, you stand watch while I find the keys." Myron emerged from the mule stable peering in all directions, especially above, on the lookout for drudgers. "Thieving will get us killed, Nico. This is serious." Myron tried not to imagine the bloody spectacle of his death on Megan's stage if they got caught.

The door on the refuser shed squeaked when Myron opened it. Entering the darkness, he led with his hands to avoid running into a rake or the points of a pitchfork. A chain tickled his nose. When he pulled it, dim yellow light spread across the room from a bulb hanging from the ceiling. Through the veil of dust, he spotted on the shelves a half-eaten pork strap, some hoof pass in a jar with mold growing on top, and a leather bag full of tools. He spread the pouch open to discover a screwdriver, a set of rusted wrenches, an awl, and a hammer. He cinched it up and looped the bag over his shoulder as he scanned the wall but found no keys. He assumed the refuser had taken the keys with him.

Myron turned out the light and slipped into the market alley where Nico waited behind the mule stable. "Come on, we have one shot at this."

They searched the market for the refuser crew's lamplight. When he heard voices, Myron hid, by instinct, something he'd done since the days when his mom crammed him into the potato bin to hide from the orange shirts. The lights from the town center reflected off the stall across the alley. Myron saw a face moving in and out of the shadows. He caught no details until he saw the scar across the man's eyebrow in the lamplight. He heard the refuser's raspy voice curse someone. The refuser tugged on a chain as though he pulled a mule that refused to move.

"There they are. Get ready." Myron pointed Nico to a hiding spot across the alley.

Kneeling down, Myron moved closer, staying low enough to avoid being seen. The refuser backed up, curses flowing from his mouth, and yanked the chain. Mah-ré and Gah-té stumbled out into the alleyway at the end of the chain, unfazed by the abuse of the man with the scar. They held hands and stood before their owner.

"What are you?" the refuser yelled. "Come on. Walk. Now." He slapped Mah-ré across the face with the back of his hand. Both girls stumbled to the ground and stood up again, joining hands, those not chained to the guide pole.

"Stop that." The man knifed his hand through theirs to break the hold. Behind them, the twins' mother kicked him in the bull eggs and jumped on his back. One of the twins stuck her thumb in his eye. The man groaned and threw the twins' mother off his back. She hit the wall hard behind them. The refuser pulled a long knife from his belt.

Nico hunkered in the alcove, but Myron bolted from his hiding spot. He raced across the alley, jumped a barrel, snagged his foot on the edge, and tumbled to the ground. Myron distracted the refuser long enough for Gah-té and Mah-ré to dodge his blade. Before he could slash again, Myron lifted the barrel he'd tripped on over his head and hurled it at the twins' owner, who toppled over. The drudgers in the catwalks above the market jogged to the scene of the scuffle.

Myron grabbed the twins and rolled them out of the

way as the drudgers fired two shots at random into the dark market. The refuser doubled over, bleeding. The twins' mother also dropped amid the clank of metal fragments and glass that clattered on the ground and ricocheted off the walls, shattering the refuser's lamp. Myron stayed on top of the twins. They kept still and silent until the drudgers muttered satisfaction that they'd stopped a theft in the market.

"Go get the refuser to clean things up down there," one of them said.

As the drudgers' footsteps shuffled off of the catwalk above Myron, he rushed to the twins' mother, hoping she'd only sustained minor injuries. He arrived to find her in a pool of blood, not breathing. The twins appeared behind him with Nico, holding hands, staring at her with the same expression they'd worn while eating the doughnut.

The day his own mother had died, at the hands of orange shirts instead of drudgers, he spotted her on the porch covered in a blanket. Before his grandfather could stop him, he'd pulled back the blanket. He'd sobbed and begged her to come back to him as the image of her lifeless face burned into his memory. Myron wished he could speak Gapi. He wanted to understand the girls, know why they stood there without emotion as their mother lay dead in the market, but born joined as they were, even if he'd known Gapi, Myron figured he might never understand them.

He patted the refuser's coat and belt, his hands brushing wet shards of glass and shrapnel around the man's waist. When he found a key ring, he tried all the keys in the twins' shackles until the chains fell away. Nudging Nico away from the scene, he tossed the chains behind a stall and took the twins' hands. "Let's get out of here."

CHAPTER THIRTEEN

Sindra awoke on a pile of pillows with the chain stretched as far as it would go, her tether reaching no farther than the squat hole. With only the haze of dim lamplight, she couldn't tell if it was night or day, how long she'd slept this time, or how much time had passed since she'd last seen Myron.

Watching Ren perform her duties gave Sindra no idea what life as a purchased slave or concubine would entail for her. Sindra envisioned servitude, being treated with harsh words or commanded about, whipped like a mule, but Megan had left her alone. She hadn't even spoken to her, so she kept to her pattern.

Sindra nestled in her own area on the floor, as far from Megan's favorite spot as she could get, and concentrated on being invisible. If she was awake when Megan was in the room, Sindra pretended to sleep. When Megan slept, while Ren worked on metals and leather, fashioning horrible new devices in Megan's dungeon, Sindra passed the day by staring at the ceiling, ensconced in her pillow fortress in comfort she'd never experienced before.

In the corner of the room, something Sindra could only reach by pulling her chain taut through the air, a table with four legs, each a different ornate spindle, held a pitcher of water, a stein of scog, and an assortment of food from the market, a spread that Ren, among her metalsmithing duties, was required to stock daily.

Since her chain clanked on the pole whenever she walked, Sindra approached the table with caution, only when her thirst drove her or the alluring smells of the snacks compelled her. She surveyed the lumps of blankets and pillows in the room to identify Megan, who slept shrouded in comfort.

Seeing no movement on the fabric sea, she gathered her chain and tiptoed toward the table, letting out slack with each step to keep the noise to a minimum. She poured a cup of water from a pitcher. Keeping her eyes peeled for movement, she gulped the water and panicked as a lump of rugs and pillows shifted in the center of the room. Megan's head rose up from the pile. Her face bore the marks of smeared powders, her hair a tangled mess. She stumbled to her feet, grabbed the scog, and downed the rest of the pitcher.

"I see you found the goodies." Megan pulled her hair back into a tail.

Sindra froze, staring into the bottom of her empty water cup. Her mental gears churned as she tried to interpret the tone in Megan's voice, wondering if she should prepare her body for a strike, the way she did before a discipline rod in Jonesbridge. But Megan wielded her control a different way than the ghosts in Jonesbridge did.

"Let's have a look at you." Megan eyed Sindra front to back, top to bottom, and gave her a swat on the backside. "You are quite a lovely. Tonight. After the show, it's time we have a session in the rumpus room."

Sindra had scrapped with the railwalkers and fought the ghosts. She had battled with women and men, taking her struggle near to her last breath more than once, but never had her flesh grown cold just by standing near someone. Megan struck Sindra with fear of a spiritual kind, as though too much time spent with her would rot Sindra's soul to its withered core. But Megan had revealed a weakness that Sindra could exploit. She would try anything to avoid the rumpus room. "I take it you've tried your toys on a witch before?"

Megan turned her back to Sindra. "Not knowingly, but it sounds delicious." She narrowed her eyes at Sindra. "Nice try, but I'm not afraid of anything, my pet."

Unlike Sindra, Ren had no chain to restrict her movement. When Megan strode off into an adjacent room Ren wandered over to Sindra, clutching a leather strap. "I don't know how long she'll keep you around. But let's get this straight now. I am Megan's girl. Not *you.*" Ren tapped the leather strap on her arm. "You're...I don't know...a disposable plaything."

"You can have her."

Ren lifted Sindra's chain and followed it all the way up to Sindra's waist. "I am the smart one around here. The pretty one. Not *you.*"

"Tell yourself whatever you want."

"What are you trying to say?"

"Smart, sure." Sindra shrugged.

"I'm just as desirable as you are." Ren glared at Sindra.

Megan came back into the room. She sauntered by her primping table and grabbed a handheld mirror. "Ren. Look at you." Megan held the mirror inches away from Ren's face. "Now." She turned the mirror so that both Ren and Sindra could see Sindra's reflection. "Look at her."

Sindra, like most Jonesbridge slogs, had avoided the mirror in her domicile. Covered in tarnished blotches and cracks, it had revealed her reflection piecemeal, a mouth here, an eye there. Megan's mirror spared no detail. It amplified them.

"While you, my dear Ren, are devilishly clever," Megan nodded to Sindra, "*she* makes my water boil." Megan stroked Sindra's cheek with her fingernail.

"I'm smarter than you think I am." Sindra jerked away. "I taught myself how to read."

"Enough. I won't have my pets fighting." Megan snapped her fingers. Ren trotted to her side with the palette of face paints, combs, and brushes for the hair and for the face powders. "What did we use to get that blue last night?"

Ren knelt beside Megan and began to paint her toenails.

As Sindra pulled her chain, she heard a noise on the other side of the wall. She held her tether still and cocked her ear. It sounded like whispering. While Megan occupied herself with her own reflection, Sindra ambled toward the sound.

"Sindra," a voice whispered.

She moved as close as she could until the chain stopped her short.

"Sindra."

"Rounder?"

"Open the door." Rounder had found a way through the secret entrance. "Hurry."

Sindra stood on one foot and stretched her arm toward the door, an inch shy of reaching it. "I can't get to it."

"Hurry. We don't have much time."

"What are you doing over there, my pet?" Megan snapped her fingers. "Get away from that wall." She pointed toward the pole.

"I was just admiring your chamber."

"Has my pet not yet learned to hold her tongue? Perhaps I shall cut it out."

Sindra ambled toward the pole, keeping her ear toward the secret passage. She could still hear Rounder, muttering curses, some she recognized, others in a foreign tongue.

"Megan," Rounder called.

The tapestries on the wall muffled Rounder's voice, but Megan heard it. She sat up straight and dropped her brush. The moment of quiet stillness, of anticipation, waiting for Megan's response, reminded Sindra of the singing of an E'ster piss whistle, guessing how close it was and where it would explode.

"Whoever's job it was to block that passage dies tonight." Megan motioned to Ren for her to open the secret door. Megan picked up her hairbrush and hurled it in Rounder's direction, where it struck the wall, shattering the bone handle.

Rounder hurried into the room. "I just came from the road."

Megan rolled her eyes. "Oh, not another warning, *please*."

Rounder took a deep breath. "I want you to listen to me."

"Listening to you has," she held up two fingers, "caused a panic on more than one occasion."

Sindra's eyes trained on the open door with excitement. She expected to see Myron stroll in after Rounder to replace her anxiety with dreams of lonely islands. Myron's absence hit her gut with a sharp pain. Nico wasn't there, either.

"The Alliance has mobilized. I saw the convoy from Jonesbridge."

Hearing the name Jonesbridge made Sindra shudder.

"A convoy, you say?"

"Everything they've got. They've even fabricated some sort of...mechanized steam walker."

Megan returned to primping for the show. "What a fabulous tale, Rounder."

With Megan's back turned, Rounder lowered the curtain over the main door to block the view of the drudgers guarding the hallway.

"Megan! They have enough firepower to turn this place into a burning heap. They mean it this time."

Megan waved Rounder off with her free hand. "You've only just returned, and I'm already getting tired of yo—"

Rounder clutched the iron pipe he'd smuggled in his shirt. He pulled it out and swiped Megan across the head. She wobbled and collapsed onto a pile of pillows. He rushed to a hook, grabbed the key, and freed Sindra from her chains.

"Rounder?" Ren gazed at him in disbelief.

"Ren, your choice. Come with us or stay here and burn."

Ren knelt beside Megan and touched her face. She checked to make sure that she still drew air.

"She's as bad as the worst of them, Ren. After what

she did to those Jonesbridge cockrels, they'll show no mercy here."

Free of her chain, Sindra ran to the table, chugged the water, and shoved as much food into her mouth as she could while Rounder urged her to the door. "Is Jonesbridge really coming?" Bits of food sprayed from her mouth as she spoke.

"They're comin', all right."

"Where's Myron?"

Ren walked backward, eyes still on Megan, and shouldered past Sindra to leave with Rounder.

Megan had blocked the passageway, but Rounder knew the way. "Close one hole, open another." They traversed a tighter passageway than before, but managed to find a new way out, with Rounder twisting through cracks and under debris.

"Chasm knows how long Megan's going to be out, but she'll wake up with fire on her breath."

In Megan's Point, running, or even a fast walk, was often mistaken by drudgers at their posts as signs of a thief making a getaway. "Walk fast, with business purpose. Not with panic."

In the catwalks above the market, drudgers walked their beats as usual, unfazed by Rounder, Sindra, and Ren striding through the alleyways to Ktala's stall.

"Get the merchants to the tunnels. Hurry," Rounder said.

"What are you on about?" Ktala made her way from the clay oven behind her stall.

"The Alliance is coming."

Ktala gathered her stock, three remaining doughnuts, and gave one to each of them.

"*Now* you have doughnuts?" Rounder shoved the pastry into his mouth. "Ack. What kind is that?"

"I'm calling that flavor prairie fire. Do you like it?"

Rounder spat the remainder of his bite into his hand when Ktala looked away. "That's a good name for it."

"Only so much I can do without the confectioner's powders."

Rounder threw his hands in the air. "What are you waiting on? Tunnels. Hurry, before Megan wakes up."

"Too late." Ren pointed toward the market security catwalks. Megan had mobilized the full drudger battalion.

Rounder took Ktala by the arm. "Let's go." They skirted the view of drudgers fanning out over the market. Ktala led them to the weaver, who raised the loom while glaring at Rounder, who was about to break the one rule of the tunnels: go only at night. The weaver uttered something in Gapi and opened the manhole cover.

"What's he saying?" Sindra whispered.

"He said we're going to get everyone killed. I told him if he was smart, he'd follow us down."

"This isn't one of your—"

"No it's not, Ktala. This is it. They are coming."

Ktala exchanged glances with the weaver as Sindra and Ren climbed down the ladder first, followed by Rounder. The entrance began to close as the giant loom came down to seal the entrance.

"Ktala!" Rounder cupped his hand around his mouth to yell.

"What is it?" Sindra asked.

"Aunt Ktala. She stayed."

"Why?" Sindra asked.

They emerged into a very different tunnel than the one Sindra remembered. Instead of people gambling, conversing, and trading under the smoky haze of torchlight, during the daytime the tunnel was empty and dark, echoing each footstep.

"My Aunt Ktala's had that bakery stall as long I can remember. Since even before Megan showed up, when this place was a den of thieves and dishonest business."

Sindra and Ren followed Rounder to a fork where the tunnel branched in three directions. "Megan wasn't always so bad. You and Myron remind me a bit of how me and Megan…used to be."

"You and Megan?" Ren smiled. "Jasper, Rounder, whatever your name is. You're just another toy with her hand up your back."

"At least I'm not her property." Rounder kept moving. "Doesn't matter now. Megan's drudgers won't stand a chance against Jonesbridge. She deserves to roast for all the bad she's done. But it won't be the same out here without her."

Rounder inspected an inscription on the wall. "Ktala said there was two ways out. I'm guessing the other way comes up outside of town." He held the torch to the symbol on the wall. "That there is the Gapi symbol for sky. Probably the way out."

"Probably?" Ren asked.

"This is only the second time I've been down here. A guess is as good as I got."

"What about Myron and Nico? What if they get lost?" Again, no answer from Rounder.

As they progressed, the tunnel grew smaller and rougher, caved in in places. They traveled in silence for a while before the tunnel ended with a cascade of bricks blocking any further travel. It reminded Sindra of the tunnel she and Myron took to get to the chapel. In the center of the passageway, a rusted ladder led to a circular line of sunlight above them. Rounder climbed up the ladder and put his shoulder into the manhole cover.

They emerged into an open flat two hects from Megan's Point, far enough, at night, for the drudgers on wall sentry to mistake them for rocks.

"Rounder, I'm not going any farther until you tell me where Myron and Nico are." Worry replaced anger. She visualized one scene after another in which Myron met his demise—shrapnel from a popcap, run through with a pike, or piñata-ed on stage before a cheering crowd. She also harbored a sense of responsibility for Nico. He would never have been exiled from his home if she hadn't shown up.

"Myron?" Rounder rubbed his face. "Mouth gets the best of me sometimes."

"What does that mean?"

"Means I sort of ran him off."

"You ran him off? How? Where is he?"

"I said some things I shouldn't have."

"What about Nico?"

"Last I saw him, he was with Myron. Then I went out rounding. That's when I saw the Jonesbridge forces."

"Where is Myron?"

"My guess, somewhere between here and Mesa Gap."

"Well, that's where we're going, then."

"No point."

"Look, I flew across a gorge full of muck and E'ster blood to a village full of fanatics that cinched me up into some sort of depravity suit. I've been bought, sold, left for dead, chained to poles, and raped by Jonesbridge ghosts no-sense-in-counting-how-many times. Myron and my baby are what I have in this world. And that's it. Come with me. Stay in that sewer. I don't care." Sindra took a breath and shrugged. "How do I get to Mesa Gap, anyway?"

"There's an Old Age highway."

"Where?"

"Just over that hill." Rounder pointed west.

In the dark, the hill looked like an easy climb, but after hiking the rest of the night, as the clamor of Megan's midnight show waned, yielding to the peach hues of sunrise, Sindra gazed back down to see a formidable hill, Iron's Knob without the cliffside. Rounder stopped on top of the hill and stared at a cloud of dust rising from an Old Age highway that stretched from one horizon to the other.

"They were heading for Megan's Point. I was certain of it." Rounder sat down, still staring at the Alliance convoy from Jonesbridge snaking down the road. "I can't believe it. I was sure they were headed for Megan. But nope."

"Where are they going?"

"That way? Either the League or Mesa Gap." Rounder counted vehicles and men with his finger.

"What is *that?*" Ren joined them on top of the hill. She pointed to the head of the convoy where a giant vehicle belching smoke rumbled on track wheels.

"That is a steam walker. I got a closer look at it yesterday. Some sort of short-range artillery tank with gate-busters on the front. Those legs on the side hoist it up to fire over obstacles with accuracy. Thing's a fiery beast."

In Jonesbridge, in the Nethers, walking the rails, at

Orkin's Landing, Sindra had never seen anything that would fit that description.

"And look at all that coal and tanks of slick." Rounder pointed to a caravan of mule-driven wagons and overloaders laden with supplies. "And I'm estimatin' three hundred or so fighters down there. And enough coal to light them factories for a week. They're practically leaving Jonesbridge unguarded and unproductive. Now I've seen everything. Whatever they're after, it must be something special."

CHAPTER FOURTEEN

"What does it mean to *go shopping?*" Myron ran his finger under a phrase in his grandfather's book. "Every time this woman encounters a frustration she says she's going shopping. But it seems like an empty phrase because she doesn't do it."

Myron's grandfather reached for the book to have a look. "Sometimes strange phrases like that need some context."

Myron watched his grandfather read two or three paragraphs before the phrase. His grandfather cocked his head and turned back several pages. "Well, let's see. Where did you find this one?"

"It was in the barn under the thresher."

His grandfather read for a while before he spoke again. "Okay, I think I have an idea." He explained that not all shops were workshops, that the word *shop* had two meanings. When Myron's grandfather went out to the shop, it meant that he would spend hours tinkering in the barn, but in the

Old Age, people referred to market stalls and merchant stores as shops.

Though he'd only read thirty pages, this revelation transformed Myron's mental image of the book. Now, instead of imagining the character going to a barn with tools, he pictured her going from vendor to vendor, shop to shop. The biggest lesson he learned from his question was that he would have figured it out himself in the next chapter, when the woman conducted an actual shopping affair that involved opulent vendors of shoes and blouses of all colors and styles, another wonder of the Old Age that he wished he could have been able to see.

• • •

The highway ended where an enormous sign blocked the way. The sign lay crunched on one side, the pole that once suspended it in the air sitting by the highway buried halfway in sand and plastic and Old Age garbage that even the wind could not dissipate. The words loomed large on the highway, though not all the letters were visible. MESA V__TA SHOPPING MALL.

Mah-ré tugged on Myron's arm and collapsed. Her sister fell at almost the same time. Nico, now pallid and shivering, even in the heat, mumbled nonsense. The sun hung midday in the sky, and the wind pelted them with sand and granules of dirt. The water that Myron took on their flight from Megan's Point he'd given to the twins and Nico. Since Myron was now confident that he was a true slog, he drank slick that he discovered in a puddle, which tied his stomach in knots and made the tips of his fingers tingle until he could no longer feel them.

Myron hoisted Mah-ré over his left shoulder and carried Gah-té on his right. Their hair dangled down his back as he hiked off the highway and around the sign to see a formidable wall as tall as a hill constructed of remnants of other buildings, stones, signs, tires, bricks, railroad ties—so many incongruous elements that it tested Myron's imagination. He stumbled toward the structure underneath the wall, dropping Mah-ré twice, while urging Nico to keep stumbling forward. Another sign on the ground read: MALL PARKING.

He walked under an arch and into a burnt-out building with a crumbling ceiling where rays from the sun knifed through missing pieces of the roof. He drew closer until he saw an Old Age storefront with a sign that read GAP, and beside it another sign that read BABY GAP.

"Mesa Gap." He lowered the twins. "We're here. Mesa Gap."

Beside the entrance, a narrow door within a large gate, two men stood guard with shotguns. The guns resembled Rounder's strong arm but with shorter barrels. Above them, the city wall extended from the top of the building, and, lost in the jumble of errata that made up the wall, Myron saw turrets and guard posts scattered throughout.

One of the guards walked into the guard shack, picked up a communication device, and spoke into it while the other approached with his gun aimed at Myron. He spoke in Gapi to the twins, who did not respond, and then he inspected Nico. Myron knew that the twins had not yet croaked because he'd heard and felt their breaths on his back during the hike. The other guard emerged from the shack, and six women rushed from the entrance, each of the women on one end of a medic stretcher. They rolled Mah-ré, Gah-té, and Nico onto the stretchers and jogged them into the shopping fortress under the Gap sign.

The guard inspected Myron and held up a hand for him to wait. In a few minutes, a Gapi man emerged from the gate, pulling a cart with a small load in the back. He wheeled it over to Myron and removed a barrel. "Dosh kani." He pointed to where the women had taken the twins and Nico, then pointed at Myron. "Naaki tó." He nudged the barrel toward Myron, who realized that he'd received the payment that Rounder had spoken of for bringing people to Mesa Gap. Though he thought it strange that he was not paid for Nico, only the twins.

"Wait." Myron ran after the guard, who stopped, turned around, and positioned the barrel of his gun against Myron's chest. "Me." Myron slapped his hand on his own chest. "Inside." He pointed to the entrance.

The guard shook his head, slapping the back of Myron's hand where it bore the brand of Industry.

"I have to see Te Yah." Myron backed away, hoping the guard would lower his aim.

"Nop."

Myron picked up the small keg of water and found a place to sit in the shade. He held it up and turned the spigot. Water gushed into his mouth faster than he could swallow it overflowing onto his face, flushing his eyes and causing a flutter in his heart, so he closed it, afraid to waste too much of his precious water.

He wiped the drops from his eyes and noticed a patch of green sticking up out of a giant pot. His excitement grew as he neared it, a plant, five times the height of a shin pine, with broad leaves and a smooth trunk, the same kind of tree as in his postcard of Bora Bora. The first leaf he stroked fell off the trunk, leaving a perfect hole with a notch. He picked up the leaf. It had the texture of a buffing rag. When he reached for another, the tree toppled over the edge of the pot. It had no roots, only a painted cylindrical trunk, making it nothing more than an ornament. By the pot with the fake plant, the remnants of a freestanding wall bore the words FOOD COURT.

Lost in thought on how to approach the guard shack, Myron wandered through the area around the entrance of the Gap, stepping over tables and chairs. He circled around an enormous crater that pocked the center of Food Court. Edging up to it, he peered into the pit. As deep as the height of ten men stacked head to foot, the steep walls of the crater tapered to a rounded-out bottom filled with skeletons of Old Age mattresses. The sun bore down on the center of the crater through a shattered glass roof with a jagged edge that resembled the blade of a rock saw, heading Myron toward the conclusion that whatever had made the crater had come from the sky.

He climbed up a slope of debris to a second story that had no floor except at its edges. At the end of a wide corridor he spotted two more guards. He continued along the sides of the floor to a bridge that connected two corridors and approached the guards who aimed their weapons at him the moment they spotted him. "Te Yah. I need to see Te Yah. It's…important."

Their heads shook at the same time as if connected.

Two other guards in the wall above them revealed their gun barrels through holes in the rubble.

"Please. What about the intention ritual?"

One of the guards pointed down to the level below them.

Myron made his way back to the main guard shack, and, passing by a stall named Biro Pizza by the Slice, he spotted an old man with a long beard sleeping in an oven. He climbed over a splintered counter for a look at the vagrant. The man's eyes popped open, and he pointed a slender strip of sharpened metal toward Myron.

"I'm just…here waiting." Myron raised his arms to show he held no weapon.

"Waiting for what?"

Relieved that he and the old man spoke the same language, Myron stepped back until he lowered his blade. "I need to see Te Yah. It's an emergency."

"Te Yah, no, no." The man gathered a handful of his beard and twisted it. "He won't see you."

"Why not?"

"You're not his folk. Me either. I tried." The man swung his legs around and squirmed out of the oven. His knotted hair jutted from his head in all directions. "I figure, short of being inside Mesa Gap, right out front is the next safest place in this windswept world to be."

"But I have to go inside."

"You don't have to. You want to." The man rolled the hair on his head with one hand and twirled his beard with the other. "Big difference." Myron couldn't see the man's mouth, only the bristle of his beard when he spoke.

Myron had spent every waking moment trying to figure a way out of Jonesbridge. Now he was going to have to do the same to devise a way into Mesa Gap. If only he had his airship, he could soar over the walls of Old Age debris and drop right into Mesa Gap. A crowd would gather round to meet the intrepid aeronaut, and Te Yah would come to greet him to hear what he had to say.

If gaining entrance to Mesa Gap posed such a challenge, Myron faced a discouraging prospect of convincing Te Yah to join forces with Megan or surrender her power source. His grandfather would have called it a "fool's errand," but much of what Myron did fit that description.

"What about the intention ritual?"

"I heard about that, too. Never got a chance, just nop, nop, always nop."

Myron climbed over the counter and returned to the main guard shack where two different men stood guard. Their gun barrels lowered as he approached. "I need to speak with Te Yah. Please. It's an emergency." Myron made a cradle with his arms and rocked. "Must save baby. Baby?" he said again. "Please."

One of the guards pointed in the direction of the road, while the other waved Myron away.

"Nop," Myron used their word. "Nop. I'm standing right here until I see Te Yah."

The two guards glared at Myron while he stared into the black holes of the gun barrels pointed at him. They remained that way for an hour, until one of the guards lowered his gun and entered the guard shack. He spoke into the communication device and returned to assume the same posture as his partner.

After a few minutes, two new guards emerged from the gate, grabbed the shotguns, and took up the same position as the guards they'd relieved, while the other guards went inside, speaking in Gapi and laughing.

Myron wondered: were they laughing at him, the pathetic Industry slog begging for entrance, standing in the line of fire of two weapons that could shred his flesh at this range? Myron's knees began to ache from standing, so he sat down, the gun barrels following his change in position. "I need to speak with Te Yah," he said again, rubbing his face. "Please."

Myron rested his head on his hands and imagined Sindra and her baby here with him, negotiating passage on an oceangoing ship bound for Bora Bora instead of trying to gain access to whatever lay beyond the barricade of junk. He drifted to sleep with Sindra's face in his mind and awoke when he tipped over, hitting his head on the ground. He shuffled to his feet, noticing that both guards had returned to the guard shack.

When the gate opened again a woman came through with an animal on a leash. She knelt down and spoke in the animal's ear, scratched its head and untied it from the leash. The animal, resembling a coyote but with short brown hair and a thick neck, raced at Myron.

"That's a dog." Myron turned to run, but remembered all he'd read about dogs in his grandfather's books, that they were a friend of man, they were companions. The dog barked, gnashing his teeth, making Myron question his decision not to run. He stood his ground. When the dog reached him he sniffed the air and Myron, his feet and hands. He circled around him, and his tail wagged. Myron reached out a reluctant hand to feel its fur.

The woman ambled up, nodding. "This is Pyro. He's the first test. Since he didn't take your arm off, you *might* be okay." She patted her leg, and Pyro ran to greet her. "Te Yah isn't doing his intention ritual much anymore. No point, he says, but I'll take you to the fire and see what comes out."

Myron followed her not inside the gate but along the outside of the wall. Pyro snuffled along the edge of the wall with purpose, hiking his leg, sniffing again, his tail wagging. Seeing such a happy creature fritter around with abandon put Myron at ease. "Can I…pet him?"

"If he'll let you."

"Where'd you get him?"

"You like dogs?"

"I don't know."

"Well, there's a whole pack of dogs that roam the hills north of here." She nodded to the north.

Myron held out his hand for Pyro to sniff. He eased his hand down onto his back. The dog's hair was coarse when rubbed toward his head; rubbing the other way, it was soft.

"Strange, he does seem to like you. Some folks he wants to tear apart."

They continued up a metal staircase across the roof of a crumbling building to a tall ladder. She put up a hand in Pyro's face, snapping a command in Gapi, compelling the dog to sit.

Myron followed the woman up the tall ladder to a turret, independent of the main structure. From here, he could see forever to the south and east, but he was still not high enough for a glimpse inside Mesa Gap. She instructed Myron to sit near a circular fire pit, and headed for a door on the other side. She pressed a button beside the door and said something in Gapi into a communication portal.

The door opened. A hand holding a leather pouch

poked out. She took the pouch and shut the door before she gave it to Myron. "Eat that."

Myron stuck two fingers into the pouch and pulled it open until it exposed a brown mass. "What is it?"

"Beast's breath." She nudged his arm with her knee. "Eat it."

Myron sniffed the bag, noting that it smelled like wet earth. He pinch the mass and shoved it into his mouth. On first chew, the texture reminded him of rubber, until it broke into moist chunks.

"Now what?"

"Wait there until the sun sets." The woman threw several gnarled shin pine logs from a stack into the fire. She adjusted kindling under the logs and lit a fire with a flint striker. "Te Yah was born blind. But he can hear deception. He may not like what you have to say, but do not lie."

With his eyes not straying from the infant fire, growing, spreading, discovering the course to take for fuel in the veins of the wood, the passage of time escaped him. Myron noticed that he was now alone. The flames expanded, shrank, and popped, in a yellow-and-orange embrace that reached for a star field above him, dripping with tears of the dead. What he'd eaten from the pouch had stolen his ability to interpret the world around him.

The door on the other side of the fire pit opened. Myron's vision blurred at the edges, the light forming long lines like legs of a star. A cane landed, a staff consisting of the skull of a small animal, the perfect size for a human hand to grasp, mounted on a section of quarter-inch rebar. A foot stepped. The cane landed again. Someone sat across the fire from Myron, silent for a period of time Myron could not measure.

"I am Te Yah," he finally said. "I am descended from the Navajo people. As the animals, forests, and fish disappeared, so have the Navajo. As the last of their kind, I have failed my people. I have been separated from their traditions, but their blood still dwells within me."

Myron saw a face in the fire, his grandfather's face, speaking the words of Te Yah before a river where bears clawed fish in a waterfall and the Superintendent of Industry set fire to the water.

"No matter what the conquerors of the Old Age brought—guns, gifts, religions, treaties, or disease, their intentions remained constant. My ancestors lost access to the land, they lost their way of life, and their language died long before the calamities that brought the world to the brink of destruction. What remains of their blood resides in Mesa Gap, along with the tongue the Gapi speak that carries a few expressions native to the Navajo. Here we welcome all heirs to the blood of great native peoples of the past."

Whenever Te Yah said the word *tongue* Myron stuck out his own tongue as if to lick the fire. His body and mind parted ways, one heading for a place called Navajo, the other digging a hole where the Gapi buried their dead.

"Hear me. There are two ways to fail this test." Te Yah drew a line with his cane. "Tell a lie." He drew another line. "Or, tell the truth and reveal your intentions to be unacceptable. Do you understand?"

"Yes."

"See the colors within the flames. Among the yellow and orange. Find the red. The blood of the animals. Wolf, bear, eagle, snake, owl, all lost forever. Which animal do you carry?"

Myron hoped to carry them all. Each bore importance and curiosity. After finding his inner coyote in Jonesbridge, he was certain he would have chosen coyote, but Coyote Man's betrayal clouded the coyote's image for Myron, sending him back to his childhood. "Elephant."

"Elephant?" They both remained silent as the fire crackled, until Te Yah spoke again. "Why elephant?"

Myron found it difficult to speak the words his mind produced, so his responses popped out in short bursts. "Strong. Gentle. Intelligent. Memory."

Te Yah threw a handful of red dust into the fire. Myron sat up when he heard the sizzle of rising flames and saw the twinkle of tiny lights. "Why do you want to enter Mesa Gap?"

Myron realized that the only reason he wanted to enter Mesa Gap was to speak to Te Yah, and there he was. "I need your help."

"My help?"

"Sindra's baby. Megan will help if you join—against Orkin."

"Join with Megan?"

"Need help in fight against Orkin."

Te Yah anchored his cane and labored to his feet. "We have constructed this fortress city so that we no longer have to fight. The earth is ill, but it will one day heal. What remains of the Navajo in the Gapi will inherit the lands taken from my people and once again thrive—in concert with the earth. Not in opposition to it. Mesa Gap will be our last reservation." Te Yah limped toward the door. "Is this the only reason you have come?"

Myron longed to speak at length about the need for new life in the world and to say that Sindra's baby could help usher in a new world. He wanted to speak with Te Yah about his salvage skills and to tell him that he would be a valuable member of their community, but the words, if they left his mouth, got singed by the fire.

"Sindra's a slave. I can buy her freedom with energy source—that you stole from Megan." Myron ran his hand through the top of the flames, his pain manifesting into enthusiasm. "Energy source that will light the night sky."

"I did not steal it—but it is true. I took the energy source from her as a responsible steward of my people. It belongs to the Old Age, not to Megan. A person like her with such power would certainly destroy what's left of the world."

"Orkin's Landing stole Sindra's baby. I don't know how to get her back. Megan said you are the only one who can challenge Orkin."

"We have never been aggressors. We will not start a war that will endanger what we have built."

Myron reclined, lying on his back to stare at the sky. Light from the stars formed streaks as he rocked his head back and forth. The beast's breath began to draw the words from deep within. "I too am a dying breed. An experiment. A mistake. A slog. My life is only worth what I am able to share."

"The twins you brought here. Where did you find them?"

"Rounder found them. With their mother. A dead man. Locomotive."

Te Yah stoked the fire with his cane. Sparks joined the

stars in the sky where Myron searched for Sindra's star. Did she still have it? The cries of babies echoed through his ears as though a hundred infants floated on the edge of the turret.

"The twins tell me that you were chained to a dead man when they found you. Is this true?"

"Dead."

"I'm sorry, Myron. Your intentions do not meet with the good of Mesa Gap."

"Wait. Please." Myron rubbed his eyes, trying to focus on the ancient man standing by the door. "I know how to read books. I have knowledge that others don't. I can salvage, too."

"I did not say your intentions weren't honorable. I said they did not meet with the good of Mesa Gap. You were found chained to a dead man. Misfortune and death will follow in your wake. Our struggle is difficult. The weights of one man's misfortune must not be heavier than that of the village. Such an imbalance leads to destruction." Te Yah reached for the handle of the door and opened it. "The twins must also return to you. Although they share the blood of noble ancestors, they were separated when they should have remained joined. One person cut in two. The boy is ill. He may stay."

"Please, Te Yah. Help me get the baby."

"We have babies in Mesa Gap. We can't risk our future for a baby in Orkin's Landing. That would make me a bad leader. Unlike the settlements of my ancestors, Mesa Gap will not be taken."

Te Yah opened the door. Mah-ré and Gah-té came out, and the door closed behind them.

CHAPTER FIFTEEN

Sindra had lost her family at such a young age that she relied on her imagination to fill in the features of their faces. She'd never met her father, one of any number of Alliance soldiers awaiting passage on the river, but she knew him—not a ghost of Civility like those who ravaged her in Jonesbridge, but a conscripted kid, torn from his home, searching for affection in the arms of Sindra's mother, a carpie. Both her grandparents suffered from toxicity and chronic wet lung, mind-addled wanderers who squandered everything her mother earned servicing soldiers' desires. Before she meandered away from home for the last time, her grandmother told Sindra that her mother's beauty drew people to her, but her eyes kept them there. Sindra couldn't remember her mother's eyes, and she often questioned what about them captured those who looked into them. Clear, wet, colorful, bloody, teared from sand and smoke—these characteristics came first to mind when she looked into the eyes of most people she encountered. But a certain life behind them, a dream that passed from one person to another in the form of a gaze—Myron's eyes held that description. When Myron held her in his eyes, Sindra's mind cleared. She worked with purpose and planned, believing in herself. His eyes gave Sindra a place to dream.

"So, what's the plan?" The only plan Sindra could devise—go to Mesa Gap and find Myron, but, seeing the force the Alliance was sending that way, she knew it wouldn't be easy.

"No one out here can stop them." Rounder nodded. "Not with that firepower. The only way we can defeat Jonesbridge is to do it while they are mobilized." Rounder headed down the hill toward the end of the caravan.

"What are you doing?" Ren asked, not following.

"I have a plan. We'll go to the League."

"Who is the League?" Sindra asked.

"A group of settlements banded together under one flag for protection," Ren said.

"Their leader is a slippery lud. Always tries to cheat me when I bring things around to trade." Rounder motioned for everyone to get lower as they descended the hill, growing closer to the Alliance convoy. "So we can't trust them to help us fight."

"Why go the—" Sindra slid on a loose rock. Her voice cracked.

"We tell the League that Jonesbridge is unguarded. That their forces are out here. That's all. They're sneaky, so they'll send their fighters to loot Jonesbridge while it is vulnerable." He snapped his fingers. "And that weakens Jonesbridge. A weak Jonesbridge helps us."

"We can't make the League on foot, Rounder." Ren crawled down to a rock to stay out of sight.

"Look there." Rounder pointed to a wagon full of coal lagging behind the faster vehicles in front of it. "That mule train is as least a mule short for the load." Rounder held up two fingers. "One driver. One guard." He put up three fingers. "Three of us. We'll dump the coal and make a run for it."

"Sounds like suicide."

Rounder glared at Sindra. "Got a better idea?"

"You were wrong about where they were going the first time. Maybe we follow them in the wings. See exactly what they're up to." Sindra had learned on the rails how to trail someone, staying within earshot, hearing conversations and plans, sabotaging, tricking and frightening those they followed. If they stayed at a safe distance, they could devise a trap, but if they went anywhere with a wagon, it should be to Mesa Gap, both to find Myron and to warn the Gapi.

"I want Jonesbridge to go down, Sindra. I thought you did, too."

"I do. But the best way to do that is to warn Mesa Gap."

"Mesa Gap won't talk to us. So we won't to talk to them."

"Ren? What do you think?" Sindra nudged her shoulder.

"Rounder's right. You may as well warn that rock over there. It'll listen to you more than Mesa Gap will."

Outnumbered two to one, Sindra recalled the game of chance that slogs played in the Swill Pen in Fourteen C. If she couldn't convince them, she could make a wager. "Let's play a game of nub. I win, we follow, unseen, to Mesa Gap. Ren, you win, we go to hijack an Alliance coal wagon, and if we are still alive, we go to the League." She held up her hand at Rounder. "It's a two-man game. You're out."

Rounder laughed. "You chose wrong. Nobody is a better gambler than Ren." He shrugged. "Except for Megan. But whatever we do, we have to hurry."

Sindra drew a two-by-four grid in the dirt. She gathered four stones, and arranged two in the squares on Ren's side of the grid and two on her end of the grid. "One move per turn. First to get both stones to the other's starting position wins."

"I know how to play. But in Megan's Point, we call this game sucker's punt."

Sindra went first, a diagonal move of her left stone, recalling the strategy she'd learned in the Swill Pen.

Rounder kept his eye on the Jonesbridge convoy. "If Myron hadn't given away my telescope, along with every other thing I had, I might be able to see what's going on down there."

"Yeah, well if Myron hadn't given it all away, I'd be stuck with those cockrels in Jonesbridge." Sindra countered Ren's move. With each turn, Ren blocked Sindra's strategy. In Jonesbridge, no one would ever play her because no one could beat her, but, as she slid her first stone into position on Ren's home side, Ren slid her second stone onto Sindra's.

"The League it is. Let's go get that wagon." Rounder began the trek down the hill.

"Sorry. I never lose at games. Except when I let Megan win. That's more of a survival tactic than a game strategy, though." Ren followed Rounder sideways down the hill.

"I never lose either." Sindra wanted a best two out

of three, for her pride, and to keep from getting killed or captured by Jonesbridge defense forces.

"Ren, you and Sindra position on the other side of that embankment." Rounder pointed to a cliff that jutted out next to the road. "I'm going to the other side of the road. We'll attack from both directions at the same time, take out the guard and the driver, and stop the mules."

Rounder dug through his pack and pulled out the pipe he'd smacked Megan with and two jagged shanks. Sindra and Ren each chose a shank.

He cycled through several confusing signals: one for attack, another for wait, yet another for stop, all involving his thumb pointing one way or another.

"We have to take them both out. No survivors. I'll take the driver. You two get the guard."

Keeping low and out of sight, they traipsed over a ridge and into position. Now that they were close enough to see the details, the Jonesbridge firepower cast shadows over any hope that anyone could put up a fight against them. Sindra counted three mule-driven tanks. Twelve bull-nosed overloaders with cannon turrets, five troop transports, two wagons loaded with piss whistles, long-range artillery, and the machine Rounder called a steam walker. The amount of coal and slick they brought made one thing clear: Rounder was right. Jonesbridge had shifted priority from production in isolation to risking everything for something out here in the wasteland of the Nethers.

The convoy left a cloud in its wake. One mule wagon with coal passed. Rounder gave a sideways thumb.

"That's go." Ren started for the wagon.

Sindra grabbed her arm. "That's wait."

"No, it's not."

"Yes, it is. Look, here comes another wagon."

Ren stopped her attack and shot Sindra a sideways glance.

Hunkered in the shadow of the ridge, they watched five coal wagons roll by, Rounder giving each a thumbs-down. When the last mule-drawn wagon in the convoy disappeared into the cloud kicked up by the machines, a single wagon rattled by, the driver urging the mules. The guard was pushing the wagon from behind as though he could help it go faster.

"This is too easy," Ren whispered.

Rounder flashed a thumbs-up. Sindra ran for the guard as Rounder instructed, but Ren made for the driver. When the guard spotted Sindra he reached for his weapon lying on the coal. In the corner of her eye, Sindra saw the driver fall. She drew her shank, but as her eyes met the guard's, eyes the same age as hers, Sindra froze. He was a prisoner in life as scared and expendable as her. She couldn't bring herself to run him through with the shank as Rounder and Ren had pounced on the driver. Rounder climbed over the coal stack toward the guard. Ren ran around the wagon from the other side.

"Sindra!"

Rounder stumbled on the pile of coal. He slid down. The mules brayed. The wagon wobbled and lost a wheel, sending the load and Rounder cascading into Ren and under the heap. The guard ran toward the convoy as the mules broke for the ditch by the highway, dragging the wagon by one wheel.

"What are you doing? He's getting away."

"So what?" Sindra screamed. "What are they going

to do? Stop their attack to track down some bandits in the Nethers?"

"It was the easiest plan. All you had to do was take out the guard." He pointed with both hands to the broken wagon wheel. Rounder chased after the mules. "And I thought Myron was a disaster."

"You know what, Myron would have come up with a plan that didn't involve killing anyone."

Rounder unhitched the mules from their center pole. "Hurry."

They each mounted a mule, without time to remove the mules' collars or bridles, and trotted off the road in scattered directions. The remaining mules ambled up the road.

Sindra pulled the bridle on the mule's right side, but the animal did not change course, trotting in the opposite direction from Rounder and Ren. The quick trot, the bounce of the mule's gait, up and down, sent Sindra toppling off her mount. She hit the ground in a flurry of dust. "Rounder!" Sindra chased Rounder and Ren on foot while her mule continued in the other direction.

Startled by the steam whistle of an overloader, Sindra looked up to see a scout team doubling back to the hijacked wagon. Rounder galloped up behind Sindra. He dismounted and helped her on his mule before they rode to the valley on the other side of the road.

He shook his head the whole way, cursing under his breath, half in Gapi. "What is it about you and Myron? What a team you make. A two-slog destruction duo, Chasm-bent on getting everyone killed that's big enough to die." Rounder kicked the mule to keep her going. He loaded up on breath to continue his tirade. "How are you still alive? I don't kill for

Megan, but that don't mean I ain't still trying to survive. And it sure doesn't mean I got a problem killin' a Jonesbridge cockrel. We could've had a wagon. A mule team. Could've made our way to the League without any problem. These mules are not accustomed to riders. They don't do well, you see." He struggled to guide the animal in the direction he wanted her to go. "And sometimes they'll take to stopping. Just like this. For no good reason."

"What? You've never messed up a plan? I only kill when I have to. And back there I didn't have to."

Ren trotted up beside them. "Forgive her, Rounder. She's the pretty one. *Not* the smart one."

Sindra reached over and grabbed Ren's sash. The mules brayed, circling away from each other.

"Enough of that." Rounder sliced his hand through the air. "Mules are getting uneasy."

They rode for a while in silence, trotting down the dirt path toward Hardsalt, the settlement where the League commandant had set up operations. According to Rounder, he trained and ran his militia the way an army trained. Each member of the League's coalition villages sent boys and girls between the ages of fourteen and eighteen to spend four years in defense corps. But only three of the original seven settlements remained, and Rounder was confident that they would coalesce into one big town to make their defense more manageable. Megan, Rounder claimed, had gotten a taste of their force when she tried to bring them her leadership a couple of years ago.

After two days of riding, stopping, riding again, and urging the mules forward, Rounder stopped at a sign with two people shaking hands next to a skull and crossbones.

"Hardsalt just up ahead. First thing we gotta do is get these mules some water."

As they approached, Rounder held his hand to his forehead to shade the sun. Smoke slithered into the sky from fires that dotted the horizon. He pointed to deep ruts in the ground, wider than the path. "Overloader tracks."

"But they were headed for Mesa Gap. It's the other direction." Ren hopped off her mule to inspect the tracks. "These aren't overloaders. They're mechanized artillery. Long range."

"They brought *two* convoys?" Rounder joined Ren to study other tracks beside the path.

"I didn't think Jonesbridge had this much in their arsenal," Sindra said.

"They don't." Rounder studied the smoke on the horizon, fueled by the structures in Hardsalt. "These weapons ain't just out of Jonesbridge. It's coming from the front lines. Back from the war with the E'sters."

"Out here? Why?"

"Ren, you been with Megan a while. What is that energy source she's talking about? The one she claims Te Yah stole from her."

"I don't know for sure. It's Old Age tech she found buried in a vault. I didn't go with her that time." Ren squinted toward the sacked settlement of Hardsalt. "My guess is Jonesbridge aims on taking Mesa Gap and that power supply for a new order, one without coal."

"Mules need water. We need water. I told you we should've gone to warn Mesa Gap. We can't go to Hardsalt now." Sindra threw her arms in the air. "They haven't left it unguarded."

Rounder tugged on the mule that refused to move. He started down the path on foot. "We can't stay here. We have to see what's left of Hardsalt. And yes, Sindra, that means you might have to do some killin'. You got a problem with that, stay here, and die with the mules."

"The only thing I got a problem with is you talking to me like I'm a kid."

Sindra and Rounder stood opposite each other at an impasse over what course of action to take, opportunities to flee ticking away with no resolution, until Ren began shouting. "They're coming!"

CHAPTER SIXTEEN

Myron awoke to a smoldering fire pit, flames dead, coals still white. Mah-ré and Gah-té sat across from him, staring out across the void of the Nethers. After Myron's eyes adjusted to the morning light, his mind not fully cleared from the ceremony, he climbed down the ladder that led from the ceremonial fire pit to the place called Food Court.

He searched for the old man who slept in the ruins of an Old Age vendor stall but found only a burlap blanket, a single shoe without a sole, and a pipe full of charred billet thistle. Myron jumped when he turned back to see the twins standing right behind him. They held hands and stared up at him as though Myron would know what to do next.

"They threw you out, huh?" Myron didn't know how much of his language they understood, but he wanted to talk to someone.

The twins stepped forward when he stepped forward and moved back when he moved back.

"Don't take it personally. At least you got to have a look inside." Myron burned with curiosity over what lay beyond the guarded wall, a settlement with entry standards and ideals, preserving civilization. His intentions—rescue Sindra's baby and liberate Sindra—did not align with Te Yah's. These were selfish intentions, Myron admitted, but he had not lied. For that, he should have been allowed at least a peek inside, but that would only tighten the pinch of being denied entrance.

"What's it like?" He pointed to the wall that rose into the sky above Food Court. "Inside." He motioned again with both hands. "Mesa Gap?"

The twins chattered in Gapi, stretching their hands high above their heads. Their eyes grew wide as they described Mesa Gap. Mah-ré drew a circle in the air and Gah-té formed a triangle with her arms. Mah-ré found a rusted piece of wire and bent it back and forth until it snapped in the middle. She kept one half and handed the other to Gah-té. They dropped to their knees at the same time and began to scribble in the dirt, one completing the image on one side that the other began on the opposite side. They operated as a machine, and when they finished, they looked up to Myron and nodded at what they'd drawn.

He joined them on his knees and studied what they'd managed to draw in the dust. Lines going back and forth, circles—he couldn't make out any of it, except squiggly lines. "What is that?" he put his finger on a string of circles.

The twins opened and closed their hands many times, an action Myron could not decipher. He struggled to interpret what they described through their gestures and floor drawings.

"What can we eat around here?" Myron made an eating

motion, putting imaginary food to his mouth, chewing on air.

The twins exchanged glances and spoke the same word at the same time in an identical tone. "Wat."

"What?"

"Nop." The twins bit their lips, produced a gnawing chatter, and brought their ears to a point. "Wat."

"Rat," Myron said. "But what do *they* eat?" To trap a rat, he would need to know what attracted them and where to find one. He curled up his hand and put it to his eye like a telescope and searched the ground with a shrug. "Where are they? I haven't seen any rats."

Mah-ré pointed with her left hand and Gah-té with her right, in the opposite direction of the rising sun to a barren valley between two plateaus. The twins again put on their best portrayal of a rat and acted as though they were eating something small, then pointed again at the valley. The landscape brought to mind another rodent that lived in such places—not quite a rat, something his grandfather called a hole bobber. The holes they dug left mounds, and their heads popped up over the mounds and bobbed back down again, a difficult meal to capture.

"Let's go." Myron snatched the old man's burlap blanket from the vendor stall and rummaged through the garbage heap in Food Court for a pipe. He knew of only one technique for snagging a rodent: cover and pound.

The hike to the valley took longer than Myron anticipated, but, as they reached the plateau, he caught a sight that made him forget his hunger and all of his other travails. A pack of dogs, the ones the gate guard with Pyro had mentioned, scrapped for a single hole bobber. He spotted big dogs and small, some with fluff and others with short hair, some wiry, some fast, and some clumsy. They barked and growled, sticking their noses into the scrum when one of them emerged from the pack with the prize in its mouth. It was the tiniest of the bunch, not much bigger than the hole bobber. She had big ears and a nose that tapered to a point. She was a dog in miniature, with hair so short it resembled suede.

The other dogs chased after another hole bobber, while the short-legged scrapper sat to feast on her prize. As Myron approached her, she dropped the bobber carcass and growled, showing her teeth. "That one's yours. I'm not going to take it from you."

Myron reached down to touch her, just to feel her coat, and, without thinking, grabbed the dog around the ribs and picked her up. The dog squirmed and bit the soft flesh between Myron's thumb and index finger. She flipped over in his hands. Myron bobbled the small dog, as if he'd grabbed a hot piston for assembly. The dog bit him again before Myron dropped her, head first, and she did a roll and skirted off in a circle.

The flat lines that formed the twins' mouths stretched into smiles before Gah-té erupted into laughter.

Mah-ré also laughed. "Th—that," she tried to speak Myron's language while pointing at the dog that circled back around for the hole bobber. "That—a *wahwahjita*." The twins chased the tiny cur back toward Myron. Blood trickled from his hand where the dog had bitten him. He watched the twins interact with the dogs and couldn't recall a time lost in such abandon that nothing else mattered.

The twins continued their chase as some of the other

dogs returned from the pack and tried to steal the hole bobber back from the little one. As Myron went for another dog to pet, one with a thick, matted coat, the ground trembled beneath him. A thunderous crack pierced the air. The ground rumbled again, and the sky in the direction of Mesa Gap filled with a rising column of smoke that blackened the morning sun. The percussive blasts reminded Myron of the drums in the anthem of the Alliance.

The pack of dogs scattered, whimpering. The biggest one cocked his head and pawed his ears when ordnance whistled overhead. The feisty little wahwahjita that had left teeth marks on Myron's hands ran in circles between Myron and the twins, barking.

A piss whistle rose from just on the other side of the hill. It zoomed through the air in a high arc before landing short of the inside of Mesa Gap. The resulting explosion rocked the wall, sending some of the garbage used to construct it cascading into the decimated roof of Mesa V__ ta Shopping Mall.

Myron grabbed the twins by the hands and ran back toward Mesa Gap. Then he saw the Jonesbridge assault force crest the hill, heading straight for them, the first wave consisting of armored overloaders equipped with raised bulldozer blades.

Most battles between settlements and clans took place at close range or with small weaponry such as shotguns and popcaps, arrows, or blades made of jagged scraps, with rifles and catapults as the only long-range fire power. Only armies boasted long-range artillery, so the fire that Mesa Gap returned came from their rifles, and struck the armor of the Jonesbridge advance. *Ping, ping, ping,* Mesa Gap's bullets connected with nothing but iron before falling to the dirt with a thud.

The protective barricade around Mesa Gap, more of a circumscribed heap than a wall, reached more than three stories toward the sky and stretched around farther than Myron could see. Within it was enough Old Age scrap to stock the Jonesbridge salvage yard for twenty years, a whole city's worth of junk. At a distance, it resembled a patchwork mountainside. Up close, the broad base that spilled out at the bottom made approaching the wall an exercise in rock climbing just to get started.

Midway up, reinforced guard posts contained spring-loaded catapults, and artillery-sized crossbows that hurled large objects from the wall onto the battlefield. The first of these that Myron saw was a big white rectangle, an Old Age machine for keeping food cold, arcing from the wall, falling, faster and faster, crashing with a *plunk* onto an overloader, where its doors popped open and it rolled over. Next up, an Old Age automobile carcass shot from the wall. It hurtled through the air to hit short of its target, but after it landed, it tumbled into a group of Jonesbridge foot soldiers, scattering some, crunching others.

Myron and the twins sprinted toward Mesa Gap. Navigating debris, he hurdled a broken concrete bench. With his attention diverted by a coin-operated carnival ride with the distorted face of a plastic horse melted into a shopping cart upended over it, he tripped and fell. The twins darted through the skeletons of stripped automobiles in the parking area adjacent to the Gap. Gunfire sounded from hidden spots on the wall above them, but both guards at the gate lay dead under a heap of rubble caused by the attack.

Myron ran for the gate. The outer gate was locked, the inner gate barred shut. "Let us in. Please." He rattled the bars.

Myron picked up a shotgun one of the gate guards had dropped and searched for shells in the fallen guard's clothing. He loaded the shotgun. A whoosh sounded over his head. High up the wall, a blast shattered a battlement, sending four Gapi fighters tumbling through the sharp debris on the wall, collapsing the gate opening, and filling it with impassable junk.

Myron prepared to fight what came next, but when a low rumble climbed up the hill and surfaced on the plateau, he froze. It was unlike anything he'd seen, a war contraption, a retrofitted steam shovel on track wheels, over two stories tall, equipped with two shovels in front inverted to claw instead of dig. It led with a locomotive snowplow that deflected anything that got in its way. On a third arm was a well-driller fitting with the capability to drill sideways, and two lifts on the side that looked as though they could elevate the machine, but Myron doubted whether it could work under the weight of the extra armor. The contraption wasn't pretty, clearly having been fabricated with parts from a few different steam shovels, but it looked as if they'd designed it specifically to bust through the Mesa Gap wall.

Myron heard the bullets coming from Mesa Gap striking the contraption again, achieving nothing more than pocking the surface of the armor. Overloader bulldozers accompanied the contraption on both sides, heading to different spots on the wall. And, between those, Myron saw that the little wahwahjita had followed them. She darted in front of the giant contraption, skirting the track wheels that almost squished her to goop as she ran toward Myron and the twins, barking.

Myron picked up the dog, which did not bite him this time, and urged the twins toward Food Court, to the safest place he could think of to hide—the crater. They slid down the steep wall of earth and out of sight. The dog jumped out of Myron's arms and trotted around the edge of the hole, making noise.

"Shhh," Myron held his hand out for the dog to sniff it. The tiny dog with the heart of a coyote had followed them into battle. She was a fearless companion. "Drillbit," Myron said, naming the dog after the first thing he thought of that was small, with a bite, and straight to the point.

The sounds emanating from the wall made the hairs on his arms stand. He climbed up the crater wall high enough to see what was happening.

The steam shovel arms of the contraption extended, shovel blades facing down like a claw, digging into the Old Age debris that formed the wall. The metal on metal screeched, plastic crunched, glass popped, concrete blocks scraped like fingernails over slate. The sound ground into Myron's ears the way it chewed up the wall. As it progressed, Myron realized why the roof of the contraption formed a steep slope: to deflect the falling debris as the wall fell apart above it.

Myron's grandfather once told him that there was a time to fight for his life and a time to run away, but there was also a time to stand up for someone else, a principle or a person, something that mattered in the world, and Mesa Gap mattered. Te Yah, the last of his kind, mattered. This wall and what lay behind it mattered, but it no longer mattered that Myron wasn't allowed inside. He understood it now. He grabbed the shotgun and climbed out of the crater to find a close-range spot that would provide him cover. He looked back to warn the twins what he was about to do—but they were gone.

While Drillbit dug into some soft dirt at the edge of the crater, an overloader rammed its bulldozer nose into a section of wall near Myron. He ran up, taking the operators by surprise from behind and fired two shots into the open back of the overloader. He yanked the driver out by his orange—now bloodstained—shirt.

Myron had never operated an overloader before, so he studied the controls, two steering levers and a steam lever, a directional control. Normal operations required an operator to drive the vehicle and a fireman to stoke the fire and shovel coal into the firebox when needed, but it had already built a good head of steam.

Myron engaged the steam. The overloader smashed into the wall. He found the directional switch and cranked it into reverse before engaging the steam again. He pulled the right lever. The rear of the vehicle went left into a concrete pillar, the impact knocking his shotgun onto the floor. He engaged forward, heading toward the giant contraption now eating away at the Mesa Gap gate.

The two-story gate crasher had armor in the rear and sides, making it impossible to commandeer as he had the overloader. Myron planned to ram it from the side, in hopes of toppling it over. He built up speed as he approached. The legs on either side of the contraption extended, making Myron aware of their purpose, to stabilize the top-heavy construction of the gate crasher.

Rapid gunfire tinked off the front of Myron's vehicle, ricocheting over his head. He peeked through the vision slit in the front armor. Bullets pinged off his water tank, rupturing it. Steam blasted from the vent and the water gushed out below the tank, bringing Myron's counterattack to an abrupt a halt.

He took a deep breath, reloaded his shotgun, and looked to the heavens, wondering if there really was a Great Above that would welcome him. The bullets kept popping off the front of the overloader. Myron gazed through the vision slit, awaiting his opportunity—then he spotted the twins.

They knelt behind the giant wall eater, out of sight of the advancing forces coming up from behind. Mah-ré hopped up onto the left-side track and squatted while her sister followed on the right-hand side. They each wielded a jagged shard of broken glass. They walked along the track wheels, squatting, and slipped, unseen and unheard, under the armor as though they were made of smoke guided by the wind. Within seconds, the clawing arms came to a sudden stop.

Drops of blood tricked out from inside the cab. Gah-té slipped out the side she'd entered and climbed over the steam shovel arms and through a tiny opening in the cascaded junk wall. Myron got a glimpse of Mah-ré behind her. Myron hopped out of the overloader in time to see a hundred or more soldiers following the advance, hoping to march in behind the contraption that the twins had just immobilized.

Myron gathered more shells, loaded his shotgun, and fired a first blast, then a second, before reloading again. He was close enough to see the eyes of his enemy, those who'd lorded over him only days ago, and it spurred his will to fight.

Two Alliance soldiers charged him. He whipped behind a chunk of the broken wall, letting it absorb the shot before he reemerged, firing two blasts. He fought, changing positions around the gate. Sweat rolled down his nose and mixed with the blood from injuries he'd sustained from flying debris and shrapnel. He made his way for the second story of Food Court to have the strategic advantage of higher ground, but it put his shotgun out of range.

The advancing soldiers saw him and began a climb to the second floor. Myron hurled any piece of junk he could, including the frame of an old sofa that toppled three of his pursuers back to the first level. He fired when they were close enough and fought to keep them at bay until he heard voices voice behind him.

"My-ron." The twins crawled out from a small recess in the wall. Hidden in shadows and hollows, it resembled a cave that wound through the mountain of junk. His respect for Te Yah aside, Myron knew he could not defend Mesa Gap alone, so he ran for the hole and crawled through, with Drillbit chasing at his heels. He snaked flat on his stomach, navigating his way under a fallen concrete pylon, following the twins as Drillbit scampered over his back and on ahead of him.

Once inside the wall, Myron realized that it wasn't a wall at all but a city folded onto itself where the ground had buckled, structure upon street upon store upon cars upon streetlights, heaped into what appeared to be an impenetrable mélange of city remains. The Gapi hadn't built the wall in as much as they'd claimed it, used it, filled in the bare spots, and massaged it to their purpose. In places Myron had to crawl, sometimes on his belly. Some spots required him to suck in his stomach until he thought his ribs would poke through his flesh to squeeze through the space. At times, the trek through the debris required him to climb and swing, hop and duck through and around objects, some of which he could identify, many he could not.

He wandered from cranny to crevice, afraid he'd lost the twins. Drillbit slipped under a flattened boat hull and circled Myron's legs before darting to an opening between two crisscrossed poles that tested Myron's flexibility. He emerged into a tunnel cleared through the rubble, bisected by a chain link fence the height of the tunnel that ran in both directions as far as he could see. The twins waited for him there, pointing to ladders on the other side of the fence that led up through the rubble where the Gapi defense teams reached their catapults.

When Myron approached the fence, the twins jumped in his way. "No touch," they whispered at the same time. They each pretended to grab the fence and closed their eyes, convulsing. "Zappo." Mah-ré tossed a piece of junk onto the fence, which buzzed and sparked when it hit.

The twins led Myron, who had to carry Drillbit to keep her from the electrified fence, to an upside-down staircase that they scaled with ease to a climbable part of the wall that jutted partway over the fence. They hopped down on the other side and motioned for Myron to follow. The drop wasn't that far, but it was high enough to sting Myron's ankles when he landed. From there, they ran back the direction they came from, this time on the other side of the fence, until they reached a ladder.

Myron climbed the ladder with one hand and held the squirming dog with the other until they reached the top.

Drillbit scampered off when Myron set her down. The mouth of the path turned into a road that passed a giant sculpture of a bear fashioned from concrete blocks, wire, and metal poles, leading them, at last, to Mesa Gap.

Inside the settlement, instead of the wall resembling a heap of garbage from the salvage pit, much of it had been transformed by the Gapi into artworks. Sculptures, totems, scenes, and landscapes constructed from and arranged in the junk that protected them from outsiders. Their view from the inside reflected the hybrid culture the Gapi had germinated. It was a celebration of what they knew of their ancestors and what they had created themselves.

The road ran adjacent to the wall toward the interior front gate, and from there, Myron could see Mesa Gap, a bustling city clustered around an enormous crater in the earth that resembled the one in Food Court, only wider and deeper, and stepped such that crops grew on a staircase of soil. Vines and plants also grew from hanging gardens suspended on cables that stretched across a portion of the city, providing shade while maximizing the use of limited water supply. A network of tracks, similar to those in the Jonesbridge mines, spiraled throughout the city. They provided transportation powered by electric current around the rim of the crater.

Near the gate, a large group of warriors, some armed with rifles, others with shotguns or bows, some rolling catapults, mobilized for battle. Myron hid in the shadow of a now-empty barrack that the wall guards had vacated for the battlefield. He made his way around the building and froze when he saw Te Yah standing by Mesa Gap's main gate with his ear toward the east as the warriors left. Through the clatter and commotion of the troops' departure and the percussion of artillery blasts on the wall, smoke billowing through the air with smell of melted Old Age plastics, half a hect away, Te Yah turned toward Myron as though he could see him.

To Myron, blind people tended to look nowhere in particular. Their gaze could fall on this or that without significance, but when Te Yah gripped his cane and began to limp in Myron's direction, Myron slipped to the other side of the barrack to evade the old man.

"You're not supposed to be here." Te Yah continued in Myron's direction. "How did you get in?"

Myron came out from hiding, holding Drillbit. The twins stood beside him. "I followed Mah-ré and Gah-té."

Te Yah cocked his head. He turned his ear toward Myron. "They are here? With you?"

"Yes, right here." Myron wondered why Te Yah could sense his presence but not the twins, although they were delicate of foot, as though they moved without disturbing the earth or displacing the air.

"They cannot be here, either. They are—unnatural. But I have heard word of your bravery and your fight on our behalf. It is appreciated. Though you are not welcome here, as a token of thanks, I will offer you something from our stores." Te Yah showed Myron the storage sheds filled with fruit and vegetables too colorful and smooth to ruin by eating. He examined stalls filled with mats and rugs, wheels, ore, bricks, wood, and bolts of cloth.

When Myron spotted the fabric, his mind went straight for the memory of his grandfather's airship and the one he'd built in Jonesbridge. He rushed through a door and into the storehouse, where he rubbed the fabric between his thumb and index finger. He stretched some of it out and held it to the window to see how much sun came through. While he waited for Te Yah to join him, Myron inspected the other material.

"All this stuff is too porous. Do you have any fabric like this?" Myron tugged on the hem of Gah-té's shirt, which was slick, lightweight material perfect for an airship.

Te Yah tapped around a crate with his cane and reached for Gah-té, inspecting the shirt with his fingers. "We have no fineries such as this. But"—he wagged his finger toward the far side of the wall—"there is a big roll of Old Age plastic that is not porous."

"Plastic? Can plastic be sewn?"

"I don't know. It is a scourge of the Old Age. It does not rejoin with the earth. It only occupies it."

Myron thought of Sindra, Nico, the twins, and maybe Rounder, and mentally measured the amount of fabric it would take for an airship of that size. "Is it too big to carry?"

"It's very heavy." Te Yah showed Myron the roll on the floor in the far corner of the storehouse. The clear plastic roll stretched two people end to end in length and toe to knee thick.

"Can…I also have that rickshaw?" Myron eyed a contraption by the storage barn with the front half of a bicycle connected to a two-wheeled cart with seats for two and a cargo bed.

Te Yah rubbed his face. "Okay. A rickshaw loaded with plastic. And then you will go."

Myron motioned for the twins to help him load the

plastic on the rickshaw bed, where it stuck out behind the vehicle like a long tail.

"How is Nico?" Myron asked.

"The boy?" Te Yah limped away in the direction of the street as Myron mounted his new rickshaw. "He is ill with fever. His wounds are swollen and…unusual."

"Will he live?"

"My physician has attended him, but with our casualties from battle, he will have to fight for his own life." Te Yah turned his ear toward the south. "You are all touched by darkness, I'm afraid. Your presence here has already disrupted our village. You must go now."

"But there's a battle going on. Please. These kids will get smashed out there." Myron thought of the stealth of the twins and figured they would fare better than he would on the battlefield, but they were young and frail.

Te Yah sighed. He turned around and began to walk toward an intersection where the rail tracks and the road crossed. "You may stay." He held up two fingers. "Two days to rest. That will give us time to defeat our enemies. Then you must go. *They* must go."

"What is this big hole?" Myron set Drillbit down. The dog scratched up soil with her back paws and darted through Te Yah's legs.

"This dog must also go in two days' time." Te Yah swatted at Drillbit with his cane. "Or sooner."

Myron scooped up Drillbit and tossed her in the cargo bed of the rickshaw.

"I don't know what caused these craters. There are many of them out here in the painted lands."

Myron pedaled his rickshaw cargo bike with the twins

seated in front of the plastic roll, while Te Yah ambled at a ponderous pace that challenged Myron's patience.

"Your city—it's big." All the structures bore the mark of the fallen world, constructed from the junk they had left behind. Myron's head swiveled as he studied an intricate sculpture of a waterfall made from thousands of nuts and bolts dangling on wires of different lengths, hung at varying depths so that it resembled water cascading down a mountain. "It must have been here a long time."

"No. Mesa Gap is a relatively new settlement. An experiment of sorts. Our old home was lacking the resources and safety for survival." Te Yah leaned on his cane and swept his hand across the panorama of Mesa Gap, the future of the Nethers, what he called "progress against the wind." He explained that his attuned hearing saved him from the darkness of being blind, but it had tortured him with the unending buzz of ambient clatter. "But my hearing—this is how we found our home. Five winters ago, we faced certain death. No water. No food. No shelter. Wandering. Unsure of where to lead my people, I followed the sound of a hum on the wind."

It was a shiver. If the earth were made of glass, he claimed, the vibration would have shattered it. "Others didn't hear it. How could they? I wasn't sure I did." Te Yah grinned, revealing his toothless gums. "When we came upon these ruins," he raised his cane in the direction of Food Court outside of the walls, "I not only heard it, but felt it." He tapped his chest. "Right here."

Te Yah led Myron down a path beside a set of tracks. They wound toward a cluster of structures built into the side of the crater. Above them, plants bearing fruit hung upside down from cables dripping with water. "When I found, at last, the source of the hum, Chooli, my adopted daughter, whispered to me—describing what my eyes could not see. This is a beautiful woman, she told me."

"Megan?"

Te Yah nodded.

"What was the sound?"

Between the houses that hung by a breath on the crater's wall and the tracks where carts ran on the energized rail, a set of cables stretched from the roof of a shack beside a silo. "This is what Megan asked you to retrieve in exchange for your friend's liberty."

Myron peeked inside the shack to see a bright green rectangle the size of a storage locker. Spliced wires jumbled above it, making it look like it had a head of unruly hair. Myron knew right away it was Old Age tech, but it looked brand new—unscratched, undented, no marks, and on the side a label bore a picture of a muscular man with a giant hammer that read:

THOR XDS 100—portable thorium power pack.
-portable reactor with patented Xenofoam cooling technology-

"Where did Megan find *that?*" Myron read the small text on the reactor. *Thor XDS 100 unit is equipped with dormancy recovery innovation for idle storage. Once activated, delivery is guaranteed for the life of the unit.*

"A bunker." Te Yah waved his hand to the horizon.

"Where?" Images of Old Age wonders filled Myron's mind. He thought of the day he discovered S.L.O.G.'s at the Stony Mountain facility under the Great Gorge.

"She told the truth about the bunker, but lied about

where exactly the bunker was." He pointed his cane to the dark bottom of the crater at the center of Mesa Gap. "I think she found it down there."

Myron leaned over the railing, staring down the steep incline to the bottom, where his imagination constructed an Old Age wonder.

Te Yah knelt and placed his hand to the ground. "I sense something down there. Megan has breathed life into this Old Age machine. I will not resurrect more of the same world that destroyed my ancestors' world."

"Why did you take it from her?"

"It's not that I *took* it." Te Yah revealed his gums again as his lips stretched into a wide smile. "I simply didn't let her keep it. Because of what irresponsible usage of such a power can lead to. Irresponsibility is in great part why the world finds itself wounded and bleeding now."

As they continued down a bricked road, they passed markets and neighborhoods—clusters of dwellings, constructed from usable pieces of the broken city that came before, some in boxcars strung together, others constructed from shipping containers stacked on each other, tucked into the wall. They shared common courtyards where dogs barked, children played, and people cooked over fire pits.

After they traversed the entire ring of the crater, circling back to the front gate, Te Yah led them to a lodge built from the fuselage of a crashed Old Age aircraft, the kind that had once ferried passengers through the sky to places like Bora Bora in a matter of hours. Myron had seen pictures of them in his grandfather's books. They carried the weight of two hundred or more passengers hanging in the sky with no more effort than a gliding a bird.

"You have now seen Mesa Gap. You have seen what is possible in this inhospitable world." Te Yah felt for the curtain that hung over the passenger hatch on the airplane. Pyro ran out straight for Drillbit. The dogs exchanged growls and barks, the hair on Pyro's neck raised. The woman who had led Myron to the intention ritual greeted Te Yah.

"This is Chooli. I believe you have met. She will give you each a cot. Eat and drink as you wish." He opened a cabinet with seedbreads and greens that made Myron's mouth water. They walked down the cylindrical corridor to an opening that led to a great room.

"You may wait out the battle here in this lodge. You are not to leave it. Your intentions do not line up with Mesa Gap," he said to Myron. "And, though they are flesh, they roam the world as phantoms," he said of the twins. "They are not welcome here."

CHAPTER SEVENTEEN

Scattered groups of people ran from the smoldering village of Hardsalt in all directions. Behind them, a transport wagon full of orange shirts hopped out to chase the villagers, bagging and thwacking them the same way Sindra remembered when the orange shirts came for her.

As people ran across the countryside, a vehicle headed straight for Rounder, Sindra, and Ren.

"Come on. Get on," a man yelled from the fourteen-man pedal bus with only four people on board. The rudderman bounced on the seat that extended from the rear of the bus, trying to steer it on the rough terrain. The bus didn't slow down, except under the weight of the three new riders when Ren, Sindra, and Rounder hopped on board.

"Crank for your life," the rudderman yelled.

The bus picked up speed as Rounder stood up to pedal, pumping with everything he had. "How—many—are there?" Rounder asked.

The woman in the seat in front of Sindra craned her neck back, still pedaling, and yelled "Chasm knows. Enough"—she took a breath—"to wipe out our defense before we could mobilize."

"Am I the only one pedaling this thing?" Rounder shouted, out of breath.

"What do you call what I'm doing?" Sindra sat in the seat adjacent to Rounder and didn't see the veins in his legs sticking out like hers. "I can't even tell you're pedaling."

"Everybody pedal." The rudderman steered the bus from the back to keep most of the weight distributed over the back axles. His seat jutted out from the rear and swiveled in the opposite direction of the turn. As they sped up, the bumps and ruts on the ground popped everyone up from their seats in jaw-rattling turbulence. "This here's a road bus. Don't handle so great on this bumpy ground. Hang on and keep pedaling."

The pop and whoosh of a steam wagon sounded as the orange shirts gained on them. "Halt the bus!" a voice called from the wagon called. Now close enough to reach the frame of the bus, the orange shirt extended his arm, getting a hand on the frame. The rudderman jerked the bus in the opposite direction. It swung toward a steep embankment, causing the rudderman's seat to swing around and knock their pursuer to the ground.

"Hang on." The front pedalman waved his hand toward the embankment as the tip of the bus went over.

Sindra grabbed the center bar. The bus creaked over the edge to a steep slope. The rudderman pulled a lever that disengaged the pedals, locking them so that the speed of the zoom down a hill, faster than people could keep up with, would not result in a bus full of broken ankles.

The drop took Sindra's stomach. Wind whipped by her ears. The bus frame rattled as they picked up speed. When the front right wheel slipped in and out of a rut, the woman in the seat in front of Rounder tumbled off the bus, rolling to stop near a boulder.

The velocity of the vehicle exceeded its ability to control direction. The bus's erratic movement tossed the rudderman off the back, sending the contraption careening to the right, traveling at an angle sideways, down until the ground began to level out. The rudderman chased the bus until it came to a halt at the base of the next hill.

With no orange shirts in sight, they settled in with a slower churn of the pedals, traveling without the urgency of escape.

"Where are we going?" a man near the back asked.

"Mesa Gap. That's the only place out here strong enough to turn back the Jonesbridge forces." The rudderman pulled a lever to guide them around a rock.

"They won't let you in. I don't know why all you people want to go to Mesa Gap." Rounder shook his head. "It's pointless. You may as well paint a target on your head and stand out in front of their wall as bait."

Hour after hour they pedaled, until Sindra was certain that she was the only one still making an effort. Myron needed her. She needed him. She would pedal the bus by herself if she had to. Cresting a hill in preparation for the next, most of the passengers stared at the ground deep in thought or grieving about losing their homes and loved ones in the invasion. Sindra, with her eyes on the horizon, spotted a column of smoke in the valley ahead. Where an Old Age highway dead-ended into the ruins of an ancient city, the Jonesbridge forces fanned out in the valley, bombarding an enormous wall with artillery and piss whistles.

"What is that?"

"That is Mesa Gap. And we're too late." Rounder motioned to the rudderman to turn the bus around.

Sindra began pedaling as hard as she could, sending the bus down the hill toward Mesa Gap before the rudderman could turn them.

"What are you doing? We're headed straight into battle." Rounder slapped his forehead. "Every last one of you nutcogs is cracked in the head. Can't I find one person out here that ain't turning circles in the dirt with their tongue hanging out?" Rounder held his feet up as the bus picked up speed. "And if I hadn't ever met Myron, I'd say you was the biggest walking catastrophe in the Nethers. But he got you beat by a hect and a half," he said to Sindra.

Everyone except for Ren, Rounder, and Sindra leaped off the bus to avoid running headlong into the fighting. The rudderman followed suit, leaving the three of them careening at high speed down the hill. With the pedals still engaged, they whipped around beneath Sindra's feet as she held her legs up to keep from getting struck. Rounder left his seat and climbed out onto the rudderman's chair to get control of the bus.

He yanked the brake lever as they reached the bottom of the hill, bringing them to a stop. "Turns out this bus ain't half bad. Put some fat wheels on her and she's a good replacement for Myron losing my glider." Rounder stepped down from the rudderman's seat. "Only problem is the steering mech."

Rounder ground the bus to a stop and pulled out the binocular lenses the rudderman kept for navigation. He inspected the battle, then peered up the highway.

"I don't believe it," Rounder muttered under his breath. Ren joined him at the back of the bus. "Have a look at that." He handed the binoculars to Ren.

"What the…"

"What do you see?" Sindra reached for the binoculars. The blurry landscape came into focus, bringing closer the image of Megan and her drudgers.

In every aspect of Megan's image-conscious life, she held true to her persona, even in the heat of battle. Half of her crew rode in chariots pulled by bicycles with heavy knobbed tires. Her sash billowed behind her like a cloud as her chariot navigated explosions. She fired a revolver at both Jonesbridge soldiers in the rear flank and the Mesa Gap warriors, who couldn't figure out where to fight, forward or backward. Another five drudgers followed in a wagon filled with bundles of burlap. Four of them fired bags from crossbows retrofitted as slingshots while the other prepared them for use. "What are they firing?"

Rounder grabbed the binoculars. "Oh, Chasm. Those are bog bags—charged sacks full of squat and weddle that explode on contact." Rounder eased out a nervous laugh. "The smell alone has a…demoralizing effect on the enemy."

Sindra took back the binoculars. "They're firing them at the Mesa Gap warriors and at the Jonesbridge forces." She watched a bag fly from the crossbow catapult, following its flight to a soldier where it hit his chest and popped, splattering human waste on his face and into his eyes. The bags rained down on the artillery, splashed across overloaders and equipment, wagons and soldiers, spreading sewage onto as much as possible.

Megan and her drudgers confused everyone and then held back, waiting for the Jonesbridge forces to weaken the warriors from Mesa Gap, who spread out from the wall to fight the encroaching foot soldiers.

With no more stomach for the battle, Sindra handed the binoculars back to Rounder, who watched the fighting, cursing in his now familiar way, half in words Sindra understood, the other half in what sounded like sleep talk.

"They're fighting alongside Jonesbridge?" Sindra shook her head. "Didn't think even Megan would stoop that low."

"She ain't fighting *with* them, she's battle drafting—taking advantage of their firepower."

"But be warned, I've seen her at her worst. There's nothing Megan won't stoop to," Ren said.

Rounder rested against the bus frame to steady his view. "She's getting awfully close to the fighting."

"Those bog bags are likely to make somebody mad." Sindra wished that Jonesbridge and Mesa Gap would join forces to crush whoever it was that smacked them with wet bags of human squat.

Even with the distraction of Megan and her drudgers, artillery fire continued to eat away the Mesa Gap wall, sending debris rumbling down the mountain of junk, and Mesa Gap responded as they could by slingshotting enormous objects that bounced around, over, and on top of their attackers. Sindra had no idea who to root for in this mess, except that Mesa Gap had to be better than Jonesbridge or Megan.

Eyes still in the binoculars, Rounder clenched his fist. "Pull out of there, Megan." After another explosion, the binoculars dropped, tumbling onto the lower bus frame and smacking the dirt. Rounder stood in a daze, still staring in the same direction. "No. no." He shook his head. "No. no. no." Rounder took off running toward the battle. "Megan!"

"What are you doing?" Ren chased after Rounder.

Sindra watched Ren chase after Rounder, while Old Nickel's voice in her head advised her to run the other way, to scatter, never show up as a group into a mess like the one up ahead. Old Nickel, Sindra's voice of reason growing up, still counseled her from the periphery of her doubts.

If all the railwalkers had fought together the day the orange shirts came for them, they might have fought them off. Out here, by herself, Jonesbridge on the prowl in more than one place, convinced her. This time, stay together.

Sindra tried to keep up, but Rounder ran as if his feet had sprouted wings until he reached Megan, where he stood over a mangled bicycle chariot. Megan draped over the side like a scarf on the back of a chair. Sindra and Ren kept low, but the fighting had shifted to the ridge where the Mesa Gap warriors assailed the Jonesbridge artillery.

Rounder lifted Megan in his arms and jogged toward the Mesa Gap wall.

"Te Yah! You son of a carpie. Let us in!" Rounder leaped over battlefield debris and bodies on his way to the gate. He fell to his knees, still holding Megan. Ren rushed to Megan's side, stroking her hair.

Sindra had seen people die many times, but never someone so powerful. In Sindra's mind, if anyone could have defeated the final call from the custodian spirits, it would have been Megan. And who would win the rights to escort her to the Chasm, since the gates to the Great Above would be barred shut for her? Starick would come for her, but so might Meron, the custodian for the erotic. Or would Larond, the custodian spirit of put-upon women, take pity on her and deliver her with patience? But Megan could turn them all away.

Megan's eye inched open, not more than a slit of color. "Jasper. I knew you'd come crawling back to me." She snapped her fingers with a smile. "I mean—*Rounder.* I'm fine. Just got my bell rung." She grabbed the back of her head. "But I did enjoy the ride to the wall."

Rounder's jaw clenched. He lowered his arms and dropped Megan, who hit the ground and rolled to her feet.

"But—all that blood." Ren wiped Megan's leg, which was coated in red.

"That's Jimir's blood, my meanest drudger. He will be missed."

She motioned to two of her drudgers now arriving in their bicycle chariots. "Be dears and tie up my precious pets." She waved in the direction of Sindra and Ren. "I was devastated when they got away last time."

Sindra darted in the opposite direction, but two more drudgers arrived to surround her, lassoing her feet and sending her to the ground with a thud, while she cursed herself for following Rounder and Ren. She should've scattered. She'd known better.

Megan grabbed Rounder's shirt and pulled him close, so that he could see the side of her head where he'd hit her with the pipe. "I can live with the headache, but if this leaves a mark, you'll have a bigger one." She flipped her hair over her shoulder and gathered it into a tail, twirling the end. "Look at this." She examined the wall. "Those tate lickers from Jonesbridge did my work for me."

Rounder stood on a bench and gazed through his binoculars at the battle on the hill where Mesa Gap warriors exchanged fire with Jonesbridge, artillery fire exploding into the wall with less regularity. "Once they deal with Jonesbridge, they'll be back for you."

"Oh, Rounder. You're so cute sometimes. I could just kiss you. But you'd like that, wouldn't you?" Megan ran her hand across Rounder's chest on her way to the gate-crashing steam walker. "Boys, fire this up."

Two of her drudgers removed the bodies from the cab. Rounder stepped back when he caught sight of the slain operators with holes in their throats. "Te Yah's men didn't do *that.* This was a sly job. I'd say there's somebody else out here besides you, Megan."

The gate crasher released a whoosh of steam. "Don't worry, Rounder." Megan said. "Ren, I know Rounder forced you to leave me, so I forgive you. But I'll keep you tied up until we get back."

The Megan's Point drudger crew formed a defensive semicircular guard stance around the gate crasher and Megan.

"That blind warthog can't see a thing, but he can hear a rat squat thirty miles away. Te Yah!" Her voice echoed through Food Court. "We're coming for you."

The behemoth advanced until it hit an obstacle, followed by a loud buzz and a shower of sparks when the machine severed a chain link fence in the middle of the junk wall. The operator, one of Megan's lieutenants, climbed out to inspect the situation. His foot hit the ground, and a jolt of lightning shot through his body from the earth to the handle on the cab of the gate crusher.

"Electrified fence." Megan held up her hand to the drudgers, who were eager to pillage Mesa Gap. "One thing's for sure, that fence won't be hot for long." She stepped in behind the machine. "Careful not to touch this thing until we get that hotwire off it." Megan tossed a tire onto the bent-up fence, which folded under the weight and pulled away from the steam walker. "Okay, all clear. Get through this wall."

Since the first time Sindra had seen Megan's drudgers, they'd gone along with orders, hopped to her command, killed who she wanted them to kill and applauded the loudest at her show. After watching their comrade in arms complete the circuit from the electrified fence with a jolt that fried him where he stood, seeing her have no remorse or regret about losing one of her own, witnessing her next-in-line-to-sacrifice-for-me attitude, some stepped back, some shook their heads, others froze, but they all gave her a reluctant refusal to approach the steam walker.

"Well, get going." Megan approached one drudger after another. "It's fine now." She marched back to the machine and checked both sides again, discovering that the fence needed another tire thrown on it to keep it off the machine. "Okay, *now* it's fine." She pointed at the cab. "Hop to it."

Wrists and ankles bound, Sindra squirmed to have a better look at the insubordination.

"Oh, don't make me do this myself. If I break a nail in that thing, I'll wear your throat as a bracelet." She pointed at the nearest drudger, who squinted with pain at the prospect of having his throat worn as jewelry. Megan raised her arm to grab the handle on the cab. She kept her hand a foot away from the metal, glancing to her drudgers, pushing it closer, an inch away, her hand trembling.

Megan grabbed the handle and climbed into the armored cab of the contraption Jonesbridge had built to break Mesa Gap's wall. The metal muffled her voice, but her message came through. "That's why you are the drudgers, and I am your queen. None of you taint sniffers has enough bile in your gut to do what has to be done."

The giant steam walker grumbled as Megan engaged the steam. Now, halfway through the hole, she retracted the stabilizing legs. The machine settled on its track wheels. She withdrew the claws and drill and lowered the bull nose, barreling headlong into what remained of the junk in front of her. Metal screeched as she reversed to pick up speed and rammed the gate and the obstacles around it.

Megan strode out of the opening with her hair flowing behind her. "We have our hole!" Her crew cheered. She examined the other vehicles Jonesbridge had abandoned by the wall. "Thor is heavy. We can't carry it. Get that overloader fired up."

"I don't know who we'll find to put up a fight in there. All their warriors are occupied." She held her head high with pride in her attack plan. "Load up anyway."

The drudgers reloaded their popcaps with glass and metal fragments. Some found discarded shotguns from dead soldiers.

"Rounder. You're coming with me. Can't have you tempted to set my pets free again while I'm gone."

"As long as Mesa Gap's been there, I've wanted to have a look inside." Rounder turned toward the wall and looked up. "Now that I'm here…it feels wrong. Doing it like this. With you."

"I liked you so much better before you grew a conscience. But it's just like a big pimple growing on the end of your nose." She pinched the end of his nose. "I can pop it any time I want. Just like I did before."

"Nope. Ain't going."

"Suit yourself." She flipped her hair and her hip in his direction as she turned toward the wall.

It took four drudgers to chase down and lasso Rounder. They sat Ren, Sindra, and Rounder with their backs to each other and tied them together, the rope going round and round them, cinching the three of them into a three-point human star.

"Megan." Rounder's voice was strained. "Take that Old Age tech, if that's what you're after, but don't kill none of them Gapi folks."

Megan laughed. "Oh, I only want one."

CHAPTER EIGHTEEN

Myron lay in his cot, staring at the ceiling in Te Yah's lodge. Worrying about Sindra, thinking, planning, his thoughts racing from one problem to the next, all his mental gears turning at once. He watched the twins sleep, embraced in the same cot, their eyes closed but threatening to pop open at any time. Nico, now reunited with Myron, shivered with fever in his cot, wrapped up in a blanket.

Moonlight shone through the windows reflecting off of the low ceiling. The room had windows on either side of a corner, one that overlooked Mesa Gap from the edge of the crater and the other with a view of the city gate. At night, lights along the paths and tracks transformed the city into a twinkling ring.

A pair of drainage ruts ran between structures and under tracks and paths, so that, during the rare occurrence of rain, the water would flow to an underground reservoir and through their filtration system without disrupting the foundations of the city. Proper drainage, Te Yah had explained, meant the difference between construction in the fertile soils around the crater and mudsliding down into a bath of junk and houses. Myron stood at the window, taking in the view, getting lost the possibility of finding more bastions of civilization like Mesa Gap out there somewhere beyond the Nethers, a place that would accept him despite being touched by darkness as Te Yah claimed. If—*when* he finally found Bora Bora, he would establish his own city there.

A screech from the wall shattered his peace. The sound of metal scraping metal and crunching debris, the same sound the wall eater had made before the twins stopped its progress. Myron tiptoed to the door and jiggled the handle, knowing it would be locked before he tried it. On his way back to the windows, he spied Drillbit curled up at the twins' feet. Nico mumbled in his sleep. Myron checked the windows next—barred shut.

With the noise at that wall, he expected that Jonesbridge had regrouped. The warriors of Mesa Gap, those that had survived the long-range attacks, had gone out to defeat the artillery damaging the city, but they never returned. With his eye on the wall, he watched the steam walker break through behind a fiery shower of sparks, anticipating a flurry of orange shirts and Alliance defense corps, shocked to see Megan and her drudgers fly through the opening in an overloader and chariot caravan. With all of the defenses either defeated or still fighting Jonesbridge, Megan rode through Mesa Gap unchallenged.

"Come on. Wake up." Myron jostled Mah-ré's shoulder. Her eyes opened, and she swung her feet to the ground at the same time as Gah-té, as though they hadn't been asleep.

He showed them the locked door. "We have to go." He pointed out the window.

The twins joined hands and walked to the window. They pressed their faces to the glass, exchanged worried glances, and whispered to each other in Gapi. "We go," they said at the same time.

Mah-ré put her ear to the door while Gah-té searched the room, returning with the bag of tools that Myron had taken from the refuser shed. When Mah-ré lowered her hand, Gah-té picked the lock.

Myron lifted Nico and carried him to the rickshaw. He draped him over the roll of plastic. The twins climbed into the two seats. Mah-ré cradled the sleeping Drillbit in her arms.

Myron pedaled for the gate. The combined weight of the load made picking up enough speed to climb the hill a chore. He pumped the pedals, hoping to get out of Mesa Gap before Megan torched the place. He kept his eye on the drudger crew as they raced around the other side of the crater, hollering their war cries.

The Gapi ambled out of their homes to see what was going on, unprepared for a breach in their wall. When they saw the marauders speeding down their streets, the Gapi shut their doors and windows and withdrew into their hidden places that Megan would overlook.

The rickshaw picked up speed as they reached a downhill section of the street. Myron put everything he had into the pedals, so that his momentum would carry them all the way to the hole in the gate. Speeding around the steam walker, through the hole in the wall, the plastic roll shifted, tipping the rickshaw. It spilled everyone out and rolled over Nico.

With the light of the empty guard shack, Myron searched for the plastic roll.

"Myron!" Sindra called. "Look, Rounder. It's Myron."

"Sindra?"

Myron scanned the shadows along the Food Court wall, spotting three people tied up, backs together, facing away from each other. Drillbit scampered over to Rounder, growling and barking. Myron scooped Nico up and carried him over to Sindra. "I can't believe you're here."

"Get us out of this. We can't be here when she gets back." Rounder squirmed.

Myron studied the rope, but lost sight of everything when the guard shack lights went out, along with the lights of the city. "What happened?"

"Megan happened." Rounder grunted and tugged, trying to loosen the tight grip of the ropes.

"I hear them," Ren said, her voice cracking.

Myron pulled at the rope, his fingers following it around until he located the knots.

"Hurry!"

"I can't get it that fast."

"She's coming."

Myron heard the calls of her drudgers and the whoosh from the overloader. He tipped the bundle of Sindra, Rounder, and Ren and did his best to roll them as a group.

"Ouch. What are you doing?" Ren said.

"We have to get to the crater." With the twins' help, he pushed, rolled, and spun Sindra, Rounder, and Ren to the crater, where they tumbled down the steep embankment onto the garbage at the bottom. Myron ran back for Nico, groping the ground until he felt the warm flesh. Myron hopped into the Food Court crater just before the headlamp on the overloader pierced through the hole in the wall.

He peeked over the edge to see a flashlight beam traveling the ground.

"Where are my pets?" Megan fumed, searching for Sindra and Ren. Then Myron saw Te Yah, bound and gagged next to the green thorium power pack, in the bed of the overloader, guarded by six drudgers, all with shotguns. "Find them!"

"No time." One of her drudgers, a scout, jogged in from the darkness. "Jonesbridge is on their way."

"I'm going to get you, Rounder," Megan screamed into the night. She climbed in the overloader and engaged the steam.

"Myron. Help," Sindra whispered.

He slid down the soil to the bottom, landing on Rounder's shoulder, and climbed around a mattress frame. Fingers searching the ropes for knots, he went to work untying them. As wiggle room allowed, the main ropes holding them together fell away for Myron to work on the individual hands and feet, attending to Rounder's last. By the time he had them free, they had to hunker down again.

Steam, wheels, boots, mules braying, and an army on the march heralded the arrival of Jonesbridge. Myron and Sindra held their embrace in the bottom of the crater, sandwiched between Rounder, Ren, and the twins. Nico sprawled out along the steep incline. All of them took shallow breaths. No one moved as footsteps crunched in Food Court. A beam from a flashlight hit the wall of the crater. It danced around the edge, lowering until it stopped at the stack of mattress skeletons. Sindra tightened her grip on Myron's arm as he relived the moment that she sailed away into the clouds without him, ripped away from his hand to dangle beneath the airship.

"They beat us to it," the Alliance captain hollered. "Mobilize. To Megan's Point!"

Relieved that Jonesbridge cared much more for finding Thor than they did for recovering escaped slogs, Myron relaxed. Sindra fell asleep with her head on Myron's shoulder, and when Myron's eyes shut, his mind filled with dreams of the ocean until he arrived on a distant shore with a pink horizon and an airplane fuselage lodged in the air between two trees, the perfect place for him and Sindra to raise the baby.

Myron awoke to find the twins standing at the edge of the crater and Nico nestled beside Sindra.

"Let's get going." Rounder's voice echoed off the Food Court wall.

Myron climbed out of the crater, worried about the condition of his rickshaw and plastic roll. "Rounder. Help me get this loaded." Myron situated his rickshaw and headed for the plastic.

"What is that?"

"Plastic sheet."

"Where'd you get it?"

"Te Yah let us have anything we wanted from his stores for helping him disable that nasty rig."

"He let you have anything you wanted and you chose this garbage?"

"That's right. Can you give me a hand?"

"No."

Myron struggled to get the roll back into the rickshaw himself.

Rounder returned to Ren, who stood by the pedal bus. Myron set to studying it, taking inventory of its function.

"Ren, great luck that you're here. This just might work." Myron rushed to meet her. "I have an idea. And you may be the only person in the Nethers that can make it happen." He lowered the bag of tools he'd swiped from the refuser at Ren's feet.

"You still owe me for the last favor I did you."

Myron snagged a wire sticking out from under a damaged sign that read PANCAKE HAUS and knelt on the ground to sketch out his idea. "Let's say, for your payment, I'll book you passage on the airship *Bora Bora*."

"What?"

"This guy's cracked in the head, Ren." Rounder pointed at Myron and inspected the long roll of plastic jutting from the rickshaw. "Anything you wanted? Not meat? Not rye water. Not shoes or hat or maybe a promise to help get that baby. The whole reason you came to Mesa Gap to begin with? You ask for plastic."

Myron ignored Rounder and scrawled his best rendition of the pedal bus in the dirt. "You'll need to find some supports. Ribs, like this. To bear the weight of the bus and keep the plastic off of the direct heat while it expands." He drew semicircular lines over the top of the bus, making it look like a dirigible. "Plastic will melt if it's too close to the flame." He recalled the time he tossed the fishing bob into his stove back in Fourteen C and it melted into red goop during Rolf's inspection. "In the garbage wall around Mesa Gap I've seen long white bendy pipes with this on them." He wrote the letters *PVC* in the dirt. "They're light and hollow and really stout."

"Wait, wait." Ren crossed her arms, studying Myron's diagram. "You're aiming to put this thing into the sky?"

"That's right." Myron drew an extension from the back of the airship. "And we're going to need a propeller with a high torque-gear ratio right here. Pedals'll turn it."

"A propeller?"

"You're the contraptionist, but we're the salvagers. Sindra can help you find something to twist up into a propeller. She's the best." Myron swung a proud arm around Sindra's shoulder. "Rounder, help roll out that plastic sheeting."

Sindra ran to the rickshaw and began to pull down the roll. "You just going to stand there?" She stared at Rounder.

"Now you're taking orders from this slack-jawed lud?" Rounder ambled toward the rickshaw.

"Rounder, we have to get out of here."

"He knows what he's doing," Sindra said.

"Ren?" Rounder stepped up behind her for confirmation.

"Well, it could work. I guess." Ren went to the bus and strained to pick up one end, gauging its weight. "This bus by itself weighs about as much as..." she cocked her head, squeezing her eyes shut as if to search the inside of her head for the answer. "Maybe forty or fifty gallons of slick." She counted the people. "Add six of us. Course, they can't weigh much." She nodded to the twins.

The bus was not much more than a skeleton with seats and pedals, but the sprockets, gears and chains, the axles and wheels, all those things added up. Ren estimated the length of the roll, and scribbled some calculations in the dirt. "This roll is a double bolt in length. But you'll need at least three quarters of a hect of it to lift this bus with us and the coal."

"How much is that exactly?" Myron studied the roll, hoping he had enough.

"Two hundred wide steps." Ren scratched her head. "But—"

Myron had already begun rolling out the plastic sheet. It bounced over the uneven ground as it unrolled, and Myron noticed the sheet was folded in half, making it twice as wide as expected but not nearly as long.

"It's folded. Okay, well, then, that makes it a quad bolt. Makes it twenty short steps wide. Then, one hundred wide steps long is what you need," Ren said.

Rounder stood on the plastic and started walking off the length.

"Beside it. You'll poke a hole it."

Rounder stepped off the plastic, glaring at Myron.

"How do we...sew this stuff?" Sindra lifted one corner of the plastic sheet.

"You'll have to fold the seams. And attach between the bottom rib and the top rib. You can melt the seams, but don't get the flame to close or it'll melt a hole. Just close enough for it to spread together."

Myron folded the edge of the sheet over about an inch to demonstrate the size of the folds to make a strong seam. "I know you can build this thing and get out of here as soon as possible."

"Where are *you* going?"

Myron gazed toward the northern horizon. "I'm going to Megan's Point—to get Te Yah back." Myron mounted the rickshaw.

Sindra dropped her corner of the plastic sheet and marched to the rickshaw, shoving Myron off the seat. He tumbled to the ground, then stumbled to his feet. She pushed him again, and a third time, backing him up to a washing machine full of sand with a shin pine twig growing from the drum.

"How can you even think about going back to that place?" She grabbed his shirt. "After all we've been through to get this far. We made it. We escaped Jonesbridge. We're free and on our way to Bora Bora, Myron."

Myron placed his hands on her shoulders. She shrugged them away. "Sindra." He nudged her farther away from the group. "I understand how you feel—"

"No. No you don't. If you did, if you felt like me, you wouldn't never even consider going back to Megan's Point on some suicide mission. He's an old man. He's lived his life. And—he won't help anyone else." A tear left a trail of clean skin through the dirt on Sindra's face. "Talk to me, Myron."

"Look. I can't explain it. Te Yah is special, Sindra. He's what this world needs right now. If it's ever going to survive."

"No, Myron. *You're* what this world needs. You are. You." She thrust her index finger into his sternum and then pounded on his chest with both hands, her face smeared with tears. "You. You."

Myron wrapped her up in his arms and held her close until she rested her head at the base of his neck. "I got a look inside Mesa Gap. I saw what's possible even out here in the Nethers. All those people." With his arm around her, he turned Sindra toward the giant wall of junk. "On the other side of that glorious salvage pit of a wall is a thriving city where people—families—live and farm and have dogs. They don't blast each other with shotguns or step on each other's throats. They don't have guards that thwack the citizens with rods or drudgers with their finger on the hammer, hoping for a chance to splatter someone with broken glass. They make art. Te Yah—these Gapi people—they're trying to live, not just survive. Megan took their electricity, but she also took their heart. Te Yah deserves better. They all do."

Sindra held back her tears.

"What good are dreams if the entire world has gone to the Chasm?" He pointed down the Old Age highway toward Megan's Point. "That man makes a difference."

"Okay. I get it. But why not let the Mesa Gap warriors rescue him?"

Myron lowered his eyes. "I don't think any of them made it back. If Jonesbridge hadn't seen Megan fleeing with that power source, Mesa Gap would be burning by now."

"Okay." She bit her fingernails. "I'm coming with you. We'll get him back together."

"No. You have to help Ren build this airship. This time we all make it out of here together."

"At least take Rounder. You can't go back there by yourself."

"I sure ain't going, so you're planning on going by yourself? Fightin' Megan and Jonesbridge at some sort of blood feud." Rounder sighed and gazed up in the air. "What'd I tell you about this guy? Gotta find Sindra. Gotta get an army. Gotta rescue a baby. Build an airship. Now, he's found his girl, but he's heading back into the fires of the Chasm for some old man that don't think any of us worthy to join his ranks."

"I'm *not* going by myself." Myron motioned for the twins to hop into the rickshaw.

"You're taking them? What for, bait?"

"'Cause they're—"

"I don't know what you have in mind, but you can't just use these kids for battle fodder." Rounder grabbed Mah-ré by the arm to pull her out of the rickshaw. "You ever stop to ask them—in their own language—if they want to die?"

"I'm not using them." The accusation pinched his conscience. "Well, ask them in Gapi. See for yourself," Myron insisted.

"I will. And I'm telling them what's in store for them, too."

Rounder gave his words some thought before launching a diatribe in Gapi that involved wild gesticulations and sound effects that resembled ripping flesh and explosions.

Holding hands in the rickshaw, the twins pointed to the northeast and responded at the same time. "Te Yah."

Rounder kicked up a cloud of dust. "Fine. Kill yourselves. Get killed for that geezer that don't give two squats about you."

"Just help Sindra with that canopy."

"What for?" Rounder shook his head.

"We're going to get Sindra's baby, and then on to Bora Bora."

"How you gonna get that baby without an army? I thought that was the point."

"Turns out we don't need an army, Rounder. *They* can get Sindra's baby back." Myron pointed to the twins.

"Them?"

"Yes. I believe they can." Myron rode over to the spot

where Te Yah's cane had dropped as he was being taken away, and picked it up. He stood up on the pedals to get a fast start on the rickshaw, never looking back, afraid he would see the worry on Sindra's face.

CHAPTER NINETEEN

After she and Ren laid out and folded the plastic, according to Myron's instructions, and prepared to mount it the way he had showed them, Sindra spent the rest of the morning scouring the Mesa Gap wall and Food Court for the white pipes with *PVC* stamped on them. Most of those she found were broken or had lost the flexibility that Myron described, but she did manage to find twenty-four pipes of the twenty-eight Ren suggested they use. If she found another four while searching for Ren's long list of needed supplies, she'd bring them, too, but Sindra tended to concentrate on one item at a time.

Returning with as many wire, cable, and cord scraps as she could find, Sindra was so lost in her work that she had forgotten about Nico. Seeing him there, eyes closed, curled into ball, caused her to inspect her own wounds. They had endured the binding together, been rubbed raw, the flesh under the cuffs made damp and soft, the skin around it callused.

Attend to Nico, help Ren, find materials. Sindra's tasks tugged her in all directions, rendering her unable to do anything except watch Ren turn her wrench on the bolt that held the main gear train on the bus.

"How's that propeller coming, Sindra?" Ren lay on her back under the bus, removing the drive shaft.

"You're really going to try to turn this thing into some flying death trap?" Rounder scratched Drillbit behind the ears.

Ren nodded without looking at Rounder.

"Why?"

"That's what I do. I build things." Ren rotated the back set of pedals, dislocating the chain from its sprocket. "Never made anything like this before, but—"

"Myron has," Sindra said.

"Yep. That's why I'm doing it. I think I can pull it off."

"Where did you learn…how to make contraptions?"

Ren held out her hand. "Pass me that mallet."

Sindra dug the mallet from the tool bag. Ren didn't possess the striking appearance of Megan, or her magnetic command of people, but she exuded confidence, convincing Sindra that, even without Myron here, they stood a chance at building the airship he'd envisioned.

"There's a man up north." Ren waved her hand as if to throw the mallet to the northern horizon. "Way up north. Top of the world. He claimed it used to be covered in ice. I don't know." Ren went back to work, her eyes concentrating on the sprocket cluster that determined how much work each set of pedals had to produce for one rotation of the axle. "He builds things. He taught me."

"What kind of things?" Sindra wondered if he knew any Old Age magic.

"Terrible things." Ren slid out from under the bus and hopped to her feet. "Why are you standing there? I need that propeller. And the rudder. And a lightweight bar. Nuts and bolts. And I don't have a drill, so don't bring back anything I can't punch with an awl."

"Rounder can get some of it."

"Hey, you know how hard it was to haul all that coal back here from the highway?" Rounder stepped up to Sindra. "And it wasn't easy finagling that fresh water from the Gapi, either. Now, they've gone and blocked the hole Megan made. No way back in."

Sindra turned back to Ren. "Terrible things?"

"Mechanical men. Clockworks for guts with faces made from Old Age dolls. And…human skin." Ren dropped the mallet into the tool bag. "I dream about them sometimes. Walking toward me with outstretched arms."

"Mechanical men? Do they talk?" Rounder asked.

"Sort of. Not really talk, but they make *sounds*. They do a lot of things."

"Like what?"

"Whatever he tells them. He encodes his instructions. And they do it."

The only aspect of Ren's tale that comforted Sindra was the fact that this *builder* lived way up north on the top of the world, a place she would never go, but with mechanical men marching into her imagination, Sindra longed for more detail. "What does he tell them to do?"

"Tasks. But sometimes they...malfunction." Ren wedged between Rounder and Sindra. She fiddled through the jumble of wires that Sindra had found. She picked up one of the white PVC pipes and worked a hole near the end with an awl, then doubled, tripled, and quadrupled a strip of wire, slipped it through the hole, and wired it to the bottom frame—another long section of PVC that extended out from the frame of the bus.

"I went to live with him when I was a kid. My grandmother left me there as an apprentice." Ren walked to the other side of the bus and held out her hands for Rounder to bend the pipe over to meet her, to form a rib like what Myron described. She wired the other side.

"Can you make one?" Rounder reached for another pipe.

"No. It's very complicated. His workshop has ten thousand clocks and...parts."

"That sounds crazy." Rounder helped fasten another structural rib that would form the support for their dirigible. "How many does he have?"

Ren thought about the question and hesitated. "A lot. They wait quietly in a barn."

The three of them formed an assembly line as they spoke. Ren worked holes in both ends of the pipes. Sindra wired them to the bus, and Rounder used his weight to bend them, breaking two of them, which left only twenty-two, eleven under the plastic and eleven over the top, one set to bear the weight of the airship and one set to hold the plastic in place.

With the airship ribcage constructed, Ren set about removing the wheels, certain that they would weigh them down too much. In their place, she and Sindra attached supports that extended like an upside-down *V*, shoulder high from the ground to accommodate the propeller.

"There go the wheels. I lose everything and," Rounder put his hands together as if to pray, "by divine providence, the Great Above goes and drops this fantastic pedal bus. Myron comes along. Yeah, Myron *again*." He smacked his forehead with the palm of his hand. "And now we got what amounts to a bloated boil of Old Age junk that won't even roll." He paced around the airship, wagging his finger, inspecting Ren's progress. "You know, I build things too. That desert glider, the riggings, sail, everything but that pinion steering mech, I put together. So I ain't some nifty rick that don't know a cotter pin from an ass hair."

Rounder slapped the nearest set of pedals, which would now be used to turn a propeller instead of an axle, though Sindra hadn't found a propeller yet. "As you can see, there ain't much but a seat and a hand hold. One wrong move. An adjustment. Anything. You're falling off this thing. And splat."

"We'll belt in." Ren shrugged at Rounder. "So what are you waiting for? Find something to belt us in." Then she turned to Sindra. "And how about that propeller?" She counted on her fingers. "And we need a flue to divert the heat, so we can come down. You do want to come down at some point, right? Or do you intend to sail right up to the sun? And we need ballast to balance our weight. And bellows to fuel the fire. A stoker. Coal bin."

Rounder and Sindra split up to find what they needed. She spotted so many things, a smorgasbord of junk, but nothing that would work as a propeller. They searched and worked into the late afternoon. Stragglers and survivors from the Jonesbridge attack on the League trickled into the area around Mesa Gap, disappointed, angry, and confused that Mesa Gap had already reinforced the hole the gate crasher had made and would not allow anyone entrance.

The League refugees wandered Food Court and the area by the shopping center, foraging and asking questions about what Ren was building, forcing Rounder to abandon his search for Ren's list of parts to stand guard against curious and aggressive Leaguers who'd lost their homes.

When Sindra spotted a bicycle wheel, an idea popped into her head. Sifting through a stack of splintered signs, she selected two railroad crossing signs and uncrossed the *X*s to give her four rectangular strips of metal. She placed the strips equal distances apart on the wheel, and attached them at an angle lengthwise to simulate the pitch of a propeller. It was more of a fan blade than a propeller, but it would work.

When Sindra returned, she gave Nico and Drillbit some water and delivered the propeller. While she was gone, Rounder and Ren had managed to situate the plastic over the dirigible ribcage that rose high above the pedal seats. The airship cut a dazzling image against the evening sky, where orange rays from the sun scattered through the plastic sheeting. Though Ren had beaten her at nub, and they'd skirmished over words, the airship before her earned Sindra's respect.

Ren had balanced the vehicle by moving the rudder levers to the center on a raised seat, giving the pilot a view of where they headed, now in a stable posture. To reduce weight load she'd pulled eight seats and pedal sets off, leaving six—one each for Rounder, Sindra, Myron, the twins, Nico, and herself, six pedalers and one pilot. In place of the removed seats, she'd positioned a crate filled with coal on each side, two more crates for supplies and a barrel for a place to stow Drillbit so she wouldn't squirm off the airship to her death.

With the light dwindling, they took turns sleeping and keeping watch with a shotgun Rounder had claimed from what remained of the battle. Nico slept more soundly than he had, giving Sindra hope that his fever would break soon, while the breeze rippled across the plastic, producing a sound that resembled an unfurled flag whipping overhead.

The last time Sindra flew had been both the worst day of her life and the best, leaving Myron but escaping Jonesbridge. She eyed the dark landscape, catching shapes moving, Leaguers with no place to go, but they had no appetite for a fight. Those with a spirit for battle had already been defeated or captured. After her shift at watch, she drifted to sleep with the memories of the cold air in the clouds and the dizzying heights of flight that made her stomach flutter. From the moment she'd landed, she'd longed to have another go at it. The thought of having that chance in a matter of hours kept her in a state of half sleep until she awoke to the familiar sound of shoveling coal.

Rounder stood up in the airship, loading coal into the hot stove, working the bellows, stoking, until the tips of the chunks turned white. He had the hot air diverted to the side to avoid lifting off without them. Ren adjusted the rigging where the plastic attached to the frame.

"Sindra." Ren waved when she saw her. "Let's get out of here. Something's not right."

"What is it?"

Rounder pointed behind her to a ring of people

surrounding them. "These Leaguers aim to take our airship, I think."

"But there are so many of them."

"It'll be like rats fussing over scraps if we stay much longer." Rounder patted the shotgun on his lap and climbed down. "I say we fly over the wall into Mesa Gap."

"We have to help Myron. We can't do that from inside Mesa Gap."

"Sindra, you've flown before. You'll be our pilot."

"But I—"

"Only pilot we got."

Rounder hauled Nico up the ladder and tied him to the frame. "Let's hope he doesn't fall out."

"Are we going home?" Nico lifted his head.

"We're going to get my baby back from Orkin. If you want to stay, that's your choice." Sindra climbed into the pilot's seat. "But you can always come with us to Bora Bora."

Drillbit barked from the barrel as Rounder diverted the heat into the balloon. For a while, nothing happened. Their flight began with a nudge toward the sky and back down again as Rounder stoked the coals. When the crowd saw that it worked, the Leaguer refugees rushed the airship.

"Take me!"

"Me!"

"Please, over the wall."

Now shoulder high off the ground, the airship frame was surrounded by hands and arms reaching for it. The extra weight brought them down again. Rounder slammed the butt of his shotgun on knuckles and wrists, across the heads of the grabbing, reaching, climbing horde who'd heckled their airship the night before.

"Pedal!"

Sindra pedaled. The propeller turned. Ren stoked the fire while Rounder fought the Leaguers. They rose. A man leaped for the frame, getting a grip, causing the airship to list to the right, but it continued to rise. When the man let go, the airship straightened and the ground fell away beneath them.

CHAPTER TWENTY

Myron wondered how the sensation of capture changed for a man without sight, the shocking sensation of running, of being caught, a bag slipped over the head, the impact of a rod at the base of the back, seeing the world cinched up in burlap and the lights turned out as the train car doors closed. Did the act come as a greater surprise, deliver a more powerful jolt to his heart, or had Te Yah's other senses foretold the episode?

Though Megan didn't use the same method as Jonesbridge to abduct her thralls, Te Yah's nose would have detected her stink in time to prepare his body for captivity. He would have heard her drudgers' breaths, their footsteps and whispers, as they came for him. But what toll would the rigors of bondage take on a man of Te Yah's age? Myron convinced himself that he would pedal his rickshaw until the wheels wobbled off the frame to reach Te Yah before

Megan devised a humiliating and grotesque blood sport for her superior rival.

With a strong wind from the south at his back and Myron pumping the pedals, the rickshaw made good time as it rolled up the Old Age highway, but it would not match the speed of an overloader. The Jonesbridge forces were also in pursuit of Megan and her power source, which complicated Te Yah's rescue, but Myron's plan would not work without them.

Myron feared the twins needed water, which he had forgotten to bring. He found it difficult to tell, as their faces always looked pale and gaunt with flaking skin around their mouths and eyes, but their frail appearance betrayed their capabilities. With the sun setting and no time to purify slick, Myron decided to pedal through the night while the twins fell asleep to the rocking motion of the rickshaw, hoping they'd drunk enough at Mesa Gap to last them.

Once the sun dipped below the horizon, fanning streaks of pink and purple across the sky, the air chilled beneath a field of stars, transforming the rock formations into gravestones in an endless dead yard. Nighttime in the Nethers made Myron feel as though he were the only living person on the earth.

The twins, huddled up behind him, shivering in their sleep, reminded him that he was not alone as he pedaled faster to keep warm. Every time he thought of Te Yah, his mind filled in scenes of what Megan would do, or already had done, to him. Each time he pushed the pedal around, his knees ached more. He thought of Te Yah. When his legs lost their drive, he thought of Te Yah.

He maintained the rickshaw's speed until the sun rose,

and he came upon an unexpected sight—Megan and her drudgers. Unable to outrun her pursuers, she had rallied her forces to defend their high position at the top of the ridge, to face Jonesbridge head on, and return to Megan's Point with the prize of the Nethers. Myron had prepared to pedal all the way to Megan's Point. Now he needed a new strategy, to rescue Te Yah *before* the old man took a stray bullet in the impending fight.

Myron stopped the rickshaw and dismounted. He gave the sleeping twins a gentle nudge. Their eyes opened at the same time. They yawned, one after the other, as Myron led them to a ditch beside the road where he hoped to formulate a plan.

He peeked over the edge of the pavement to see Megan striking a regal pose on the bed of her overloader, her thick mane of hair trailing behind her like a battle flag held on the breeze. Her hair was one thing she cared about. In her chamber he'd watched her brush it for an hour, gazing at it in her mirror, braiding and unbraiding it, pulling it up and letting it down. It might provide enough distraction for Myron to make his move.

From the tools in the refuser's bag, Myron dug out a knife with a bone handle and a whetstone. He sharpened the blade until he could shave the fine hairs from his arm. He pointed at Megan and faced the twins, pretending to grab a handful of hair behind his head. With the knife in his other hand, he made a shearing motion. "Cut her hair."

Gah-té reached for the knife. "Cut." She stabbed at the air.

"The *hair*." Then the thought occurred to him—why not let the twins run Megan through with the blade if they could get close enough to cut her hair? Doing so would save countless future victims from her bloody games. But one drudger he hadn't seen stepped up beside Megan, joined by three others that climbed aboard her overloader. "No, wait. That's a bad plan." Myron took the knife back from Gah-té.

"Bad plan," Mah-ré repeated.

Megan had a fleet of bicycle chariots in her caravan but only four power trucks. Those needed steam. Steam required water. He fished out two adjustable wrenches from the refuser's tool bag. Myron explained the plan to the twins the best way he could without words, by drawing in the dirt.

Each with a wrench in hand, Gah-té gave Mah-ré a slight shrug as they looked at each other, studying one another's reaction to Myron's instructions. "Got it?" He nodded toward them, hoping for a confirmation that they understood, but the twins offered only an impassive stare.

As Megan and her drudgers dug in to defend their prize, Myron took a deep breath and gave the signal, a sideways nod toward the caravan. Mah-ré and Gah-té slipped off toward the overloaders. Their ragged black hair whipped behind them like ripped burlap in the wind. Their stealth amazed Myron. They were no more noticed than a feather falling onto a pond.

Gah-té crawled under Megan's vehicle and positioned herself on her back to tighten the pressure relief valve. Myron hoped this would trigger the safety stop and disengage the drive temporarily. Mah-ré headed for the other vehicles to open the drain valve on the water tanks.

The rumble of Alliance forces from Jonesbridge sounded from the other side of the ridge. As Mah-ré sneaked to the adjacent overloader, Myron noted the steady flow of water from the tank where she'd loosened the drain, making him confident she understood the procedure. On her third and final vehicle, Mah-ré turned the wrench.

"They're coming," Megan yelled. "Let's send those taint sniffers straight to the Chasm." She gave the signal for her drudgers to flank the Jonesbridge forces as they emerged over the ridge. The drivers struggled to engage their vehicles. When nobody took their positions, Megan screamed, "What are you waiting for? Go!"

"No steam!"

She looked to the other overloaders.

"None here."

"Nope." He shook his head.

Megan engaged her vehicle. It responded with a jerk and came to a stop. Her face reddened. "Come on." Her plea was drowned by the rumble of the Jonesbridge forces breaching the ridge. She waved for all her drudgers to join her in a new plan of attack, to lie in wait, leaving the power pack as bait, to ambush Jonesbridge forces when they tried to take it.

As soon as Megan left her vehicle, Myron gave Gah-té the signal. She turned the wrench to reenable the relief valve and climbed on board. Myron ran to Megan's vehicle, which held both the power source and Te Yah. He waved Mah-ré on as she raced to join him.

Myron pulled the steam lever. He awaited the whoosh of the pressure release and maneuvered the gear to forward drive, open fully to achieve top speed.

With her eye on the ridge ahead, Megan turned and screamed when she heard the sounds of steam. She grabbed four of her drudgers and ran for her prize, slowing down only to take aim at Myron. "The only good slog is a dead slog!" she yelled as shot scattered against the back of the vehicle. Her bullets pinged against the fenders, ricocheting off the armor.

In the chaos, the Alliance troops overran the drudgers that remained. The Jonesbridge forces sped past Megan, pursuing Myron for the power source. Myron puttered over the hill, putting distance between himself and Megan, but the only way to escape the Jonesbridge forces, who drove vehicles as fast as or faster than his, was to cede the *Thor XDS* portable reactor to the orange shirts, leaving the Great Above to weep for their enemies.

Myron drove until he could hear the pursuing overloaders behind him. He stopped the vehicle, hoisted Te Yah over his shoulder, and made a run for the top of the next hill with the twins gasping behind him, trying to keep up.

Myron carried Te Yah on his back, the old man's arms locked around Myron's neck, his legs wrapped around Myron's waist. When Gah-té collapsed beside him, Myron handed Te Yah's cane to Mah-ré and tucked her twin under his arm. He toted both of them, which slowed his pace from a jog to a stumble up the hill.

Behind him, orange shirts cheered.

When Myron saw that the Alliance troops were content with commandeering the power source and had no more yearning to bag and swat people, he fell under the weight of this passengers and caught his breath, unable to run any more.

Te Yah rolled off of Myron's back with a moan. His lips puckered around his gums as he labored to speak. "Thank you for sparing me—the spectacle of death at the hands of Megan." Te Yah felt for Myron's hand and guided it to his abdomen, which seeped blood from a deep wound. "Leave me now to die here in peace on the hillside—under the sun." He lifted his hand to Myron's face and turned toward the warmth of the sun. "I'm afraid I was wrong...about you. We...could've used a man like you in Mesa Gap."

Myron placed Te Yah's cane across his chest. "I can carry you. I know I can."

"No. It is time for me to go. Chooli will lead the Gapi into a new age." He aimed his ear toward the sounds of the orange shirts. "Jonesbridge has the reactor?"

"Yes." Myron watched the overloaders putter away down the gulley back toward the highway.

"The Alliance. The E'sters. The Gapi. We all do what we think we must. Megan does what she does from vanity. She would use the power pack for sport, but the pools of blood would run no farther than the outskirts of the Nethers. With power like that, I fear the Alliance will awaken a sleeping bear that the men of the Old Age unleashed upon the world."

"I'm sorry. I didn't know what else to do."

Te Yah turned his head and stopped breathing.

Myron studied the old man's face as his spirit left him, the folds in the skin around his eyes, the wrinkles above his lips where the flesh loosened from having no teeth underneath. He closed Te Yah's eyes, imagining what bitter organs they were for a man who could not use them, the pale stare that offered nothing but mystery.

The ceremony in Richterville, when the village doyen died, reminded Myron of the importance of history and age. The story board, with its carvings, kept their legacies alive. Te Yah was himself a story board. A man who had never seen the world knew more of what it looked like than anyone. Thinking about the first question Te Yah had asked him that night by the fire pit, Myron wondered what animal Te Yah carried. In Myron's mind Te Yah carried them all—the wolf, the bear, the owl, the eagle, the snake—and the elephant. With help from the twins, Myron placed rocks around and over Te Yah's body, marking the spot of his burial with his cane.

"I see you over there! My piñata!"

Megan's voice startled Myron from his quiet thoughts. He looked up to see her and her four remaining drudgers on the other side of the gulley. Images of her entertainments and midnight rituals and the power she wielded threw his judgment off course. He nudged the twins to run, knowing that it would take Megan some time to cross the gulley. He ran behind them.

Megan watched for a moment as the power source she'd risked everything for disappeared in the distance. She stumbled down though the ravine, running faster than Myron would have thought she could for her consolation prize.

He and the twins ran with abandon, knowing the drudgers would soon be in range unless they maintained their speed. Their muscles cramping and with little energy left to run, they crested the hill to a sight Myron had only seen in dreams. An airship against the afternoon sky cast a shadow across his path.

"They did it!" He grabbed the twins' hands, raising them skyward. "They really did it!"

"Myron!" Sindra waved from the pilot's seat. "We're coming down."

"Megan's right behind me!" Myron yelled back. He had envisioned the airship, but Ren had made it possible.

His grandfather would have been impressed by the solid construction. From this view, every detail rang true to his specification. So taken by the sight of it, Myron didn't realize he'd slowed down until he saw the twins already at the airship, Rounder's arm extending to lift them on board.

Myron looked back and stumbled as the drudgers jogged over the top of the hill. They fired two shots. The shrapnel fell short of Myron. Two other drudgers fired at the airship. Some glass and metal *tinged* off the airship frame, but not with enough force to do damage. Rounder stoked the fire to gain altitude.

"Come on, Myron!" Sindra yelled.

Rounder lowered the mooring rope. It dangled from the airship, which continued to rise. The drudgers stopped to reload. Myron's legs ached. He ran for the rope, but it hung in the sky beyond his reach. He gazed upward. Sindra's face came in and out of focus with the sun behind her. Again he watched her as she rose in a flying machine without him, pursued by armed madmen. This time, he would take the bullets, the shrapnel to the face, and join Te Yah in a pile of rocks on the hillside rather than come so close again—but the rope lowered.

"I'm coming, Myron," Sindra called.

He grabbed the rope. His extra weight yanked the airship down as he tried to hang on. Rounder turned the diverter so that the heat went into the balloon and stoked the fire. Myron wrapped the rope around his hand, holding tight as he rose, an inch, a foot, the height of three men standing on top of each other. Seeing the rocks and hills grow smaller beneath him distracted him from Megan's curses that the wind carried away.

Rounder pulled as Myron climbed until he reached the frame and slid into the seat over the last open set of pedals. The earth spread out in all directions, bringing memories of his grandfather and his gift of flight.

Myron's stomach reeled at the view with nothing more than pedals and a seat separating him from a fall from the clouds.

"We did it, Myron. We finally did it." Sindra started to untie her harness. "Here, you drive."

"No. You're a natural." He thought Sindra was the right person to sit in the pilot's seat. She had a steady hand and knack for the movement of the air.

"Which way do we go?" Sindra steadied the rudder levers as everyone drove the propeller by pedaling harder.

In Richterville, as a kid, Myron's world had consisted of the Alliance, which governed everything he knew, and the E'sters that encompassed everything else. He didn't pretend to understand the complexities of politics and the competitions between rival alliances, but Te Yah had been an ambassador of peace. Out here in the Nethers, he'd seen that there was still more in the world than he'd ever imagined, renewing his hope of finding Bora Bora. But first, they would have to find Sindra's baby in Orkin's Landing, which sat at the edge of the sunset on the coast of the Great Western Ocean.

As the afternoon yielded to evening, Myron pointed toward the western horizon. "Follow the sun."

Printed in the USA
CPSIA information can be obtained
at www.ICGtesting.com
JSHW031711140824
68134JS00038B/3637